PRAISE FOR ALEX MILLER

A KIND OF CONFESSION

'A fascinating, moving account of the cost of commitment to writing, of the process, the disappointments, the sheer slog of it, the rejections, and the human buttresses who held Miller firm at his desk.'
—Morag Fraser, *Sydney Morning Herald*

'Miller is a genuinely great storyteller whose ostensibly plain narratives carry a tremendous freight of revelation and ethical understanding in many different national and cultural contexts.' —Brenda Walker, *Australian Book Review*

'This Miller is essential reading for any would-be writer.'
—Stephen Romei, *The Australian*

'Diverse and engrossing . . . a rich blend of letters and notebook extracts by one of Australia's most loved novelists.' —Sylvia Martin, *Inside Story*

'I found myself drawn into the book's lively, often thought-provoking exchanges with family, friends and readers. Its recurring preoccupations range from the domestic and homely to the worldly and philosophical.' —Brigid Rooney, *The Conversation*

A BRIEF AFFAIR

'More than one ghost haunts this tender novel about love in its many guises, condoned and illicit . . . will resonate long after its pages are closed.' —Sylvia Martin, author of *Ink in Her Veins*

'A richly satisfying and luminous novel.' —Tom Griffiths, author of *The Art of Time Travel*

'A rich landscape . . . *A Brief Affair* is a moving study of the value of both writing and reading. In many ways it is a distillation of all of Miller's invaluable fiction.' —Joseph Cummins, *The Guardian*

'This book radiates the compressed skill of Miller's long and successful career. It's a tale about love, beauty and belonging.' —Christine Kearney, *Canberra Times*

'There's a seductive, languid poetry to Alex Miller's writing that gently lulls the reader into his world and makes it a place you never want to leave . . . A masterpiece.' —Juliet Rieden, *Australian Women's Weekly*

'Miller engages profoundly with the inner lives of women . . . One of Australia's finest storytellers.' —Stephen Romei, *Weekend Australian*

'*A Brief Affair* is a quiet novel, focused on just one life. But in its emphasis on the ways we might each construct our own story—while respecting the stories of others around us—it has a profound impact.' —Jessica Gildersleeve, *The Conversation*

'Masterful . . . Elements of the novel have an almost dream-like inevitability to them, and the weaving together of seemingly disparate plot strands is immensely assured.' —Sally Pryor, *Canberra Weekly*

'*A Brief Affair* is a beautifully told tale that explores the self we present to the world, the self that changes over time and the secret part of ourselves we keep hidden from the world. It's a story about memory and experience, the compromises we make along the way, the relationships we form and the paths we navigate as life unfolds.' —*Reading Matters*

'Miller is one of our greatest storytellers . . . he does not shy away from intimate details, nor broad strokes of observation and humour. Miller holds up our follies and archetypes to consider how they react in different lights, and *A Brief Affair* is his compassionate way of exposing us all.' —Readings

MAX

'A perfectly poised autumnal masterpiece. Only a master of the craft of the novel could write a book of non-fiction of such quiet power and beauty.' —Robert Manne, *The Age*

'A successful combination of the life of Max Blatt and the gripping story of the author's search for him.' —Charmian Brinson, Emeritus Professor of German, Imperial College London

'A wonderful book. Miller is faithful to Max Blatt's story, to his silences and to his sadness. It is a story that needs to be heard.' —Jay Winter, Charles J. Stille Professor of History, Yale University

'With *Max*, Miller the novelist has written a wonderful work of non-fiction, as fine as the best of his novels. Always a truth-seeker, he has rendered himself vulnerable, unprotected by the liberties permitted to fiction. *Max* is perhaps his most moving book, a poignant expression of piety, true to his mentor's injunction to write with love.'
—Raimond Gaita, Emeritus Professor of Moral Philosophy, King's College London, and award-winning author of *Romulus, My Father*

'A long, deeply absorbing and moving detective story . . . a celebration of the way [Max Blatt] is remembered, with all the inevitable gaps and imperfections, in the lives of those who follow him.'
—*Australian Book Review*

'There is a slow, elegant circling in the storytelling, as if Miller is holding the precious shards up to the light and gently turning them to reveal their every facet . . . [*Max*] offers a deeply moving meditation on history, imagination and truth, and portrays a fascinating, visceral wrestling with facts.' —*Weekend Australian*

'A powerful, humane portrait of a man who suffered immense loss.'
—*The Age*

'A moving and masterfully written testament to the power of friendship.' —*The Guardian*

'*Max* is haunted by devastating insights . . . Miller's intelligent love has created a tale for the ages.' —*Sydney Morning Herald*

'Beautifully written, engaging, deeply human . . . a book to savour and to pass among your friends.' —*Canberra Times*

THE PASSAGE OF LOVE

'Miller's story is long, intense and vital.' —Geordie Williamson

'*The Passage of Love* is capacious, wise, and startlingly honest about human frailty and the permutations of love over time. Frankly autobiographical, it is also a work of fully achieved fiction, ripe with experience, double-voiced, peopled with unpredictable men and women, and set in Miller's landscapes that characteristically throb with life.' —Morag Fraser, 'Books of the Year', *Australian Book Review*

'Half a dozen of Miller's novels are likely to be judged among the finest of the past quarter century. They were written in the course of a career that has showcased Miller's subtlety, narrative craft, moral acuity and delight in writing about what he loves.'
—*Weekend Australian*

'Conflicting demands that can throttle creativity are a big motif in this bildungsroman . . . A thoughtful autobiographical work by an award-winning Australian novelist . . . traces themes of art and commitment through Crofts' relationships with three women. Miller pulls back from the narrative several times in interludes that return to the first person of the much older man and highlight how memory has many layers. A rich addition to the growing shelf of autofiction from a seasoned storyteller.' —*Kirkus* (starred review)

'. . . delivers an enthralling fusion of fiction and memoir.'
—Tom Griffiths, 'Books of the Year', *Australian Book Review*

'While Miller's novels are immediately accessible to the general reading public, they are manifestly works of high literary seriousness—substantial, technically masterly and assured, intricately interconnected, and of great imaginative, intellectual and ethical weight.' —Robert Dixon in *Alex Miller: The Ruin of Time*

'It is riveting and a masterpiece in every way . . . great emotional depth . . . a magnificent achievement.' —Nicholas Birns, Professor of English at the New School in New York and author of *Contemporary Australian Literature*

'*The Passage of Love* is a novel that explicitly revisits aspects of Miller's life with the aim of shedding light on subjects beyond its biographical orbit . . . a slow-burning catalogue of marital breakdown enlivened only by Miller's trademark prose, limpid and grave and stately in progression, each sentence fragment tongue-and-grooved with the next.' —*Australian Book Review*

'An intimate book . . . Miller has a gift for examining the domestic and exploring private lives.' —*Good Reading*

'*The Passage of Love* offers an insight into a great writer's journey . . . Miller maintains a tangible sense of place throughout, in particular, the landscape of isolated country NSW. This novel is a must for fans of Miller.' —*Books+Publishing*

'There is something elegiac about *The Passage of Love*, in its detailing of a vanished 1950s Melbourne, in the passion and urgency of its fierce protagonist . . . Miller's writing has the muscularity of decades-earned craft, spare and unsentimental, probing the sinews of marriage,

delineating the arc of love affairs, of struggle and disappointment.'
—*Irish Times*

'Miles Franklin Award–winner Miller has crafted a novel that's individual in its essence with originality and sensitivity.' —*PS News*

'*The Passage of Love* is a gift. It tells us about living with an undeniable creative force and the consequences of being utterly transparent in one's desires. It is an observation, a sharing of knowledge and a transcript of a life lived with yearning . . . Extraordinary.' —*Readings*

'The most candid, sharing, generous book I've read in a long, long time.' —Michael Cathcart, ABC Radio

'A great read with profound insights into the nature of love and creativity.' —*Australian Financial Review*

'An exquisitely personal life story told in a fictional style . . . Miller draws on memories, dreams, stories, love and death to create a moving and raw fictional novel that is the closest to an autobiography likely to be read from him. In a rich blend of thoughtful and beautifully observed writing, the lives of a husband and wife are laid bare in their passionate struggle to engage with their individual creativity.' —*Highlife*

THE SIMPLEST WORDS

'Most collections of this kind are interesting and useful reminders of the value of a writer of considerable literary standing. *The Simplest Words* is more powerful than that, because of Miller's intense

engagement with his subjects, and because Stephanie Miller has chosen pieces that speak to one another, accounting, in a way, for one of our most original, engagingly vehement and expansive writers.'
—Brenda Walker, *Australian Book Review*

'This is a rich, generous compilation that enticingly refracts our perceptions of one of Australia's finest novelists.' —Peter Pierce, *The Age*

'[Miller's] writing has a luminous quality that sings off the page and whether he is writing on family, friendship, memory or just life, he engages with the reader, involving them in his orbit.' —Helen Caples and Martin Stevenson, *The Examiner*

COAL CREEK

'Miller's voice is never more pure or lovely than when he channels it through an instrument as artless as Bobby . . . The intelligence of the author haunts the novel, like an atmosphere.' —Geordie Williamson, *The Monthly*

'. . . a master of visceral description.' —*Weekend Australian*

'Because of this subdued mode of storytelling, the tension mounts gradually and when tragedy strikes it is truly, hideously, mesmerising . . . an evocative and moving novel of the Australian bush.' —*Books+Publishing*

'*Coal Creek* is a story of friendship, love, loyalty and the consequences of mistrust set against Miller's exquisite depictions of the country of the Queensland highlands.' —*Books and Arts Daily*

AUTUMN LAING

'Such riches. All of Alex Miller's wisdom and experience—of art, of women and what drives them, of writing, of men and their ambitions—and every mirage and undulation of the Australian landscape are here, transmuted into rare and radiant fiction. An indispensable novel.' —*Australian Book Review*

'. . . in many respects Miller's best yet . . . a penetrating and moving examination of long-dead dreams and the ravages of growing old.' —*Times Literary Supplement*

'A beautiful book.' —*Irish Times*

'Miller's prose is so simply wrought it almost disguises its sophistication . . . The result transforms one woman's dying words into pure and living art.' —*Weekend Australian*

'. . . a magisterial work . . . a compulsively readable tale.' —*The Advertiser*

'Miller has invested this story of art and passion with his own touch of genius and it is, without question, a triumph of a novel.' —*Canberra Times*

'Miller engages so fully with his female characters that divisions between the sexes seem to melt away and all stand culpable, vulnerable, human on equal ground. Miller is also adept at taking abstract concepts—about art or society—and securing them in the convincing form of his complex, unpredictable characters and their vivid interior monologues.' —*The Monthly*

'Few writers have Miller's ability to create tension of this depth out of old timbers such as guilt, jealousy, selfishness, betrayal, passion and vision. *Autumn Laing* is more than just beautifully crafted. It is inhabited by characters whose reality challenges our own.' —*The Age*

'Miller's long honing of the craft of his fiction has never been seen to better advantage than in *Autumn Laing*.' —*Sydney Morning Herald*

'Nowhere in Miller's work has the drama of character been so well synthesised with the drama of ideas. Nowhere else have his characters drunk ideas like wine and exhaled them like cigarette smoke, a philosophical questing indistinguishable from defiant bohemian excess.' —*Weekend Australian*

LOVESONG

'With *Lovesong*, one of our finest novelists has written perhaps his finest book . . . *Lovesong* explores, with compassionate attentiveness, the essential solitariness of people. Miller's prose is plain, lucid, yet full of plangent resonance.' —*The Age*

'*Lovesong* is a ravishing, psychologically compelling work from one of our best.' —*Courier-Mail*

'Miller's brilliant, moving novel captures exactly that sense of a storybuilt life—wonderful and terrifying in equal measure, stirring and abysmal, a world in which both heaven and earth remain present, yet stubbornly out of reach.' —*Sunday Age*

'*Lovesong* is another triumph: lyrical, soothing and compelling. Miller enriches human fragility with literary beauty . . .' —*Newcastle Herald*

'Alex Miller's novel *Lovesong* is a limpid and elegant study of the psychology of love and intimacy. The characterisation is captivating and the framing metafictional narrative skilfully constructed.' —*Australian Book Review*

'The intertwining stories are told with gentleness, some humour, some tragedy and much sweetness. Miller is that rare writer who engages the intellect and the emotions simultaneously, with a creeping effect.' —*Bookseller & Publisher*

'With exceptional skill, Miller records the ebb and flow of emotion . . . *Lovesong* is a poignant tale of infidelity; but it is more than that. It is a manifesto for the novel, a tribute to the human rite of fiction with the novelist officiating.' —*Australian Literary Review*

LANDSCAPE OF FAREWELL

'The latest novel by the Australian master, so admired by other writers, and a work of subtle genius.' —Sebastian Barry

'*Landscape of Farewell* is a triumph.' —Hilary McPhee

'Alex Miller is a wonderful writer, one that Australia has been keeping secret from the rest of us for too long.' —John Banville

'As readers of his previous novels—*The Ancestor Game, Prochownik's Dream, Journey to the Stone Country*—will know, Miller is keenly interested in inner lives. *Landscape of Farewell* continues his own quest, and in doing so, speaks to his reader at the deepest of levels. He juggles philosophical balls adroitly in prose pitched to an emotional perfection. Every action, every comma, is loaded with meaning. As one expects from the best fiction, the novel transforms the reader's own inner life. Twice winner of the Miles Franklin Award, it is only a matter of time before Miller wins a Nobel. No Australian has written at this pitch since Patrick White. Indeed, some critics are comparing him with Joseph Conrad.' —*Daily News*, New Zealand

'*Landscape of Farewell* has a rare level of wisdom and profundity. Few writers since Joseph Conrad have had so fine an appreciation of the equivocations of the individual conscience and their relationship to the long processes of history . . . [It is] a very human story, passionately told.' —*Australian Book Review*

PROCHOWNIK'S DREAM

'Assured and intense . . . truly gripping . . . This is a thoroughly engrossing piece of writing about the process of making art, a revelatory transformation in fact.' —*Bookseller & Publisher*

'With this searing, honest and exhilarating study of the inner life of an artist, Alex Miller has created another masterpiece.' —*Good Reading*

JOURNEY TO THE STONE COUNTRY

'The most impressive and satisfying novel of recent years. It gave me all the kinds of pleasure a reader can hope for.' —Tim Winton

'A terrific tale of love and redemption that captivates from the first line.' —Nicholas Shakespeare, author of *The Dancer Upstairs*

CONDITIONS OF FAITH

'This is an amazing book. The reader can't help but offer up a prayerful thank you: Thank you, God, that human beings still have the audacity to write like this.' —*Washington Post*

'I think we shall see few finer or richer novels this year . . . a singular achievement.' —Andrew Riemer, *Australian Book Review*

THE SITTERS

'Like Patrick White, Miller uses the painter to portray the ambivalence of art and the artist. In *The Sitters* is the brooding genius of light. Its presence is made manifest in Miller's supple, painterly prose which layers words into textured moments.' —Simon Hughes, *Sunday Age*

THE ANCESTOR GAME

'A wonderful novel of stunning intricacy and great beauty.'
—Michael Ondaatje

'For pure delight, abandon the maze, and read for sensual pleasure. This is a gift of floors of lacquered Baltic pine, pearwood shelves and tea boxes. There is the perfume of the camphor laurel trees, coats made of the pelts of eighteen grey foxes, and Victoria Tang's horse. Smell the porridge and sour pickles, cross the cold wet slate courtyard flagstones. Remember chrysanthemums the deep rust color of an old fox's scalp.' —Sara Sanderson, *Indianapolis News*

'A major new novel of grand design and rich texture, a vast canvas of time and space, its gaze outward yet its vision intimate and intellectually abundant.' —*The Age*

'A dense, complex work that addresses the issues of cultural displacement, colonialism and the individual's imaginative link to earlier generations . . . Extraordinary fictional portraits of China and Australia.' —*New York Times Book Review*

'One of the most engrossing books I've read in a long time.' —Robert Dessaix

'Takes the historical novel to new frontiers. It is fabulous in every sense of the word.' —Commonwealth Writers Prize judges

THE TIVINGTON NOTT

'*The Tivington Nott* abounds in symbols to stir the subconscious. It is a rich study of place, both elegant and urgent. An extraordinarily gripping novel.' —*Melbourne Times*

Also by Alex Miller

A Kind of Confession
A Brief Affair
Max
The Passage of Love
The Simplest Words
Coal Creek
Autumn Laing
Lovesong
Landscape of Farewell
Prochownik's Dream
Journey to the Stone Country
Conditions of Faith
The Sitters
The Ancestor Game
The Tivington Nott
Watching the Climbers on the Mountain

ALEX MILLER
THE DEAL

ALLEN&UNWIN
SYDNEY·MELBOURNE·AUCKLAND·LONDON

This is a work of fiction. Names, characters, places and incidents are products of the author's imagination or are used fictitiously. Any resemblance to actual events, locales or persons, living or dead, is entirely coincidental.

First published in 2024

Copyright © Alex Miller 2024

All rights reserved. No part of this book may be reproduced or transmitted in any form or by any means, electronic or mechanical, including photocopying, recording or by any information storage and retrieval system, without prior permission in writing from the publisher. The Australian *Copyright Act 1968* (the Act) allows a maximum of one chapter or 10 per cent of this book, whichever is the greater, to be photocopied by any educational institution for its educational purposes provided that the educational institution (or body that administers it) has given a remuneration notice to the Copyright Agency (Australia) under the Act.

Allen & Unwin
Cammeraygal Country
83 Alexander Street
Crows Nest NSW 2065
Australia
Phone: (61 2) 8425 0100
Email: info@allenandunwin.com
Web: www.allenandunwin.com

Allen & Unwin acknowledges the Traditional Owners of the Country on which we live and work. We pay our respects to all Aboriginal and Torres Strait Islander Elders, past and present.

 A catalogue record for this book is available from the National Library of Australia

ISBN 978 1 76147 157 5

Set in 13/20.4 pt Granjon by Bookhouse, Sydney
Printed and bound in Australia by the Opus Group

10 9 8 7 6 5 4 3 2 1

 The paper in this book is FSC® certified. FSC® promotes environmentally responsible, socially beneficial and economically viable management of the world's forests.

For Stephanie

CONTENTS

A true story in four parts

The Boy   1
The Man   7
The Deal   31
The Time of Ghosts   271

Acknowledgements   281

THE BOY

1

October 1942. The boy, Andy, is six.

It was just breaking day when the father went in and touched the sleeping boy's shoulder. He leaned down, putting his mouth close to the boy's ear, and said softly, 'Come on, son, we'll take a run out to Keston Ponds.' The father was on a twenty-four-hour leave before returning to his regiment at the front. They packed sandwiches and the fishing gear and the father's paintbox and walked up the road and caught the Green Line bus. There was no one else on the bus. At the ponds they dropped in their lines and watched the floats, the father tamping his pipe with his thumb, the nail browned and split, while gazing steadily at the rippling surface of the water with its world of shadows and reflections. After a few minutes the father reached around and opened his box of materials, and father and son settled to sketching the trees and the pond and putting in clouds and there was a church steeple poking up from behind the line of trees. The boy put the steeple into his sketch but the father left it out of his. The father was more concerned with getting the effect of the light on the water, the ripples spreading out from the floats whenever they bobbed, the dark line of trees rising up behind, isolating the pond and making a private setting of it. It was surprising what you could do if you had the right pencil. The sun was well up by now and it was a fine autumn day. The two of them sitting there lost in their drawing, looking up to check the reality, the details intriguing, distinguishing one thing from another, crosshatching and shading delivering the illusion of form and substance on the page. They did not hear the distant sound of traffic; alone together they made their drawings, the father and his son, sharing their love in the silence of concentration. They were at home in themselves and at peace.

In the living room that evening, after the father and his son had cleared away the dinner dishes and washed them up, the father opened his paintbox and he and the boy made watercolours of the scenes they'd sketched earlier in the day, hunched over the dining table now, then sitting back, head to one side to better judge the effect, not speaking, the occasional settling of the coals in the grate, the mother sitting by the side of the fire darning the heel of a sock, her half-pint of stout warming on the hob, the sister lying on the rug in front of the fire reading her book.

'We must find our own style,' the father said when the boy, whose name was Andrew, asked him if what he was doing was right or not. 'We learn our way by searching for it.' It was the first thing the boy would remember being told by his father. *We find our way by searching for it.* It stayed with him after his father had gone back to his regiment, and over time it became the son's private wisdom. And there were occasions when it was the source of his consolation, and then it was art that consoled him. Not the challenge, but the deep innocence of art he had known with his father. That became his portion of sacred country. He was often lost to the world when drawing the details of a face or a rotten piece of timber with its worm holes and fungus, oblivious then to troubling uncertainties.

His father was not killed in the war but returned a changed man, wounded in his body and his soul, from which the innocence of art had been driven out. And that is how the boy lost his father. But art remained within the boy, a gift from his father. Isolated in its innocence by his loss, art became for the boy a deeper and more private thing. Gradually, over time, he became aware that he lived at the margins. As he grew into himself, so it was to the margins that he came to owe his allegiance as a writer.

THE MAN

2

2016. Andy is eighty.

Many years have passed already since his visit to me, but still I think back with a mixture of pleasure and sadness to that late summer evening before his return to England, when my brother and I sat together for the last time in the garden of the small house in the country where I was then living. Across the lawn from where we were sitting that evening there was an old apple tree. It was a tree of great character and was at that time of the year, and despite its extreme age, laden with a fine crop of ripe apples. My brother and I had been silent with each other for some minutes when he stirred himself and, turning to me, reminded me, with a kind of innocence of recollection, that there had been just such an apple tree as this one in our garden at home in England when we were children. He went on to remind me that when we were boys we would check whether the apples were ripe by holding one close to our ear and shaking it. If it was ripe, the seeds rattled. So saying, my brother returned to me this long-forgotten memory of our childhood garden. I was moved to tell him that I had been prompted in my decision to buy the house on account of this handsome apple tree that stood before us, and which had occasioned his recollection of our childhood.

'When I first came with the real estate agent to view this house as its prospective purchaser,' I said to my brother, 'the town and its location were not familiar to me. I had come to the town in the hope of finding relief from my situation in the city, a situation which had become intolerable to me. Jo had passed away the previous year and our only child was contentedly settled in Bordeaux. I hoped new surroundings and a degree of isolation from everything that had for so long been familiar to Jo and me would help restore my sense of purpose and wellbeing, and that I would once again be able to work. Although in my mid-sixties at that time, I was hoping it would be possible for me to make a fresh start. I believed I was too young to permit despair to defeat me, but was I too old to begin again?

'I arrived in the town that day on an early train and began my quest for a house buoyed by a feeling of optimism and the sense that I was embarking on an adventure. Traipsing around the town all that day with the agent, however, entering one vacant house after another, each seemingly more desolate than the last, it began to seem to me that I was following the hopeless trail of an impossible dream. As the day wore on and I gazed about me at those silent rooms, observed anxiously all the while by the real estate agent, I began to fear that I was to become a member of a caste of forlorn and anonymous refugees from reality whose melancholy fate was to roam from place to place, moved by an unnameable yearning for home that nothing was ever going to satisfy. With the loss of Jo, I had lost my home. In seeking to make a new start, was I, after all, merely in a state of denial?'

I fell silent, but my brother said nothing and seemed to wait patiently for me to finish my story.

'The afternoon was well advanced when we at last approached this house,' I went on. 'I was by then tired and dispirited and was ready to accept my defeat and to return to the city, convinced that my idea of moving to the country, which when I first conceived it I had thought to be original and uniquely my own, had in fact been nothing more than a commonplace attempt to evade my problem rather than to confront it with courage and imagination. As we drew up outside this house in the agent's car, I turned to him and said, *This will be the last house I shall look at.* I asked him if he would be kind enough to take me to the railway station on his way back to his office, so that I would be in time to catch the evening train to the city. The agent paused at the door before inserting the key into the brass lock and he said that after almost forty years of acting as a real estate agent, the sheer number of people who were not happy in their choice of house had never ceased to surprise him. He said no more but turned the key and swung the front door open and stood aside to permit me to enter.

'I had taken no more than three or four steps along the passage when I glimpsed a view of this old apple tree through the small window that looks out onto the garden from the sitting room, and in that instant I experienced a feeling of homecoming that was uncanny. I turned to the agent at once and told him I would buy the house. Catching sight of this stately old tree, its branches spreading and unpruned for decades, growing here at the edge of the lawn as if it were the patient grandparent of the garden itself, surrounded by the respectful grace of the lawn and looked up to, one might say, by the buddleia and other untended and wild-grown shrubs in the border behind it, I felt as if I were being welcomed home. Yes, it was quite uncanny. I was moved, and stepped to the window and stood gazing across the lawn at the sunlit tree with a mixture of gratitude and relief. I felt sure I had known the tree in a former, happier, life.' I looked at my brother. 'And as you have just told me, this was in fact the case. Now that you have reminded me of the apple tree in our childhood garden, I am astonished that I have never once connected it to my love of this tree.

'The agent asked me if I would not prefer to see the rest of the house before confirming my decision to purchase it. I said I was sure the house would be ideal for me. *I feel at home here*, I said to the agent, and was pleased when he seemed to understand my feelings. He said people will feel at home in a house for the most trivial and strange reasons that often have nothing to do with their descriptions to him of their ideal house. When I first glimpsed the tree through the little window from the sitting room, it was bathed in evening sunlight, just as it is now. My heart contracted at the sight of it and I knew I would be able to live happily in this house even if I were to discover that it was in every other way unsuitable to my needs. As it turned out, and as you now know, this house has suited my needs in every respect. It would not be an exaggeration to say that I have spent some of the happiest and most productive years of my life here.'

When I had finished speaking, my brother and I sat in silence once again, admiring the old apple tree; admiring its splendour at that moment, for the upper branches of the grand old tree were illuminated by the last coppery radiance of the setting sun. As my brother and I sat there, each aware that in the morning our brief time together was to come to an end, it was as if we listened to a piece of music the strains of which were so exquisite as to make us long to postpone indefinitely the moment when it would finally draw to a close. When the last of the coppery light had faded and the garden had fallen into the sombre shadows of evening, a change of light as abrupt as if a curtain had been drawn across the scene, my brother said, quite as if his remark were of no particular consequence to either of us, 'Our father received his wound while sitting under an apple tree in an orchard.'

Although at the time I could have had no inkling that this information, so casually imparted to me by my brother at the end of his stay with me, was to change the course of my life and work, a kind of astonishment at the discovery of how deeply significant the apple tree had really been for me all these years took hold of me. I said nothing, but listened while my brother went on to describe in some detail my father's situation that day long ago in 1942, when he was wounded while on active service in France.

Three months or so after my brother's return to his home in London, at the beginning of an unusually severe winter, when I was once again living alone in this house, I had put my book aside and was in the act of placing the screen in front of the open fire preparatory to getting ready for bed one evening when the telephone rang. It was my brother. He said he hoped it was not too late and that he had not woken me. 'Calling you on the telephone,' he said, 'always feels to me as if I am calling another world altogether, and I can never feel completely confident that our morning here really will prove to be your evening down there.'

I assured him that he had not woken me and that I had been on my way to bed when he rang. But all the same his words did make me feel a little as if I were living a deeply solitary existence in the underworld and he was calling me from somewhere infinitely remote and in sunlight on the distant surface of our planet. I must confess that London, which is my birthplace, has always seemed to me to be a place where life is more real, more certain and more elaborately optimistic than life can ever be in Australia, where I have lived since the age of sixteen in, for the most part, perfect contentment.

I asked after his health and he said that his health was his reason for calling me. 'You're not unwell?' I asked. My brother was eleven years younger and had always seemed to me to be the baby of our family.

'I'm not well,' he said.

I said I hoped it was nothing too serious. But even as I expressed this hope, I knew, with a fatal certainty, that my brother was calling in order to tell me he was dying.

'I have pancreatic cancer,' he said.

I permitted a small silence before responding, 'You knew of it, I suppose, when you came out to stay with me?'

He laughed, amused, as if I had made a joke. 'It was the cancer that finally decided me to visit you after all these years of only threatening to do so,' he said. 'So we have something to thank it for.'

I asked, 'Is there no chance you may recover?'

He replied, 'My oncologist—he is an old friend, David Samson, you met him during one of your visits—does not expect me to live more than a few weeks more. A month at most.'

There was an easygoing matter-of-factness about our discussion of my brother's disease and imminent death that lent to the dismal subject an almost cheerful sense of unreality. He and I had always found it easy to laugh with each other. It was as if his news did not threaten to replace our old reality with a new and distressing one but bestowed on us an additional reality that was to satisfy its existence in parallel, as it were, with the old familiar reality in which our lives were to go on indefinitely and as we had always lived them. Our emotions were masked by this peculiar matter-of-factness and neither he nor I sounded in the least disturbed by the grim subject of our conversation. Beneath this subterfuge of two realities, however, we each knew there were no words with which to describe our sadness. I had referred to him in my mind ever since my childhood as *my little brother.* Our love for each other had remained unblemished by the usual childhood rivalries. When he was very young I had left our home for good and had only revisited for short periods since, so that in our old age our love for each other still stood as a virgin field and had not suffered the usual trials and dislocations of a lifetime of intimacy.

'There's not going to be a funeral,' he said.

I was not surprised to hear him say this, for neither our mother nor our father had had a funeral. Not to have a funeral had almost become a kind of family tradition with us, the expectation being—as if it served our unwritten moral code of modesty—that we would each depart from this world in silence and without any sign of public mourning or display.

'I don't want you to come to England to see me,' he added. 'I would like to carry with me to my end the memory I have of us on that last evening of my visit to Australia, when we sat together in your garden and enjoyed the lovely spectacle of the evening light on your apple tree, as if we listened that night, you said, to the closing bars of an entrancing piece of music.'

Since his earliest years my brother had been a lover of classical music and had listened to it every day throughout his childhood with rapt joy and attention. His joy in music had been so consuming when he was very young that my parents had at one time grown fearful lest he become so deeply enchanted that his relationship with reality would become impaired. I think they saw him being swept away on the tide of an idée fixe, in which the ideal world of music displaced his ability to deal successfully with the everyday world. In fact, in his life's work as a senior manager in a large manufacturing company, my brother proved himself to be the most practical of all of us. His passion for music had never grown less but had remained his principal consolation throughout his life.

I said to him, my tone gently teasing, 'So, tell me, Harry, which piece of music most aptly fits the mood of our last evening by the apple tree?'

He laughed and did not hesitate but replied at once, 'The second movement of Mozart's Sonata for Piano and Violin in C Major. It is the andante. There are several C major sonatas. I am talking about the second movement of K296. You have it. I saw it in your collection: it is the Anne-Sophie Mutter and Lambert Orkis CD.' I heard in his laughter the joy in his mind, for no doubt as he spoke he *heard* the soulful melancholy of the work he spoke of.

I said, 'I shall listen to it before I go to bed tonight.'

'You will recognise it,' he said confidently. 'You are familiar with it.'

There was a silence during which we each seemed to hold our breath. Then, stumbling a little over our words and knowing we were never to see each other ever again, we said goodbye.

Three weeks after we spoke, my brother's wife, Christine, rang me from the hospital in London. It seemed too soon for this call.

'It is the middle of a fine summer night here,' she said, her tone perfectly even and only a little strained. 'Big Ben has just struck midnight. The young people are all still out in the streets enjoying themselves. From the window where I am standing the city is a blaze of light below me. What is it like where you are? I cannot imagine it.'

I replied, 'It is a wintry day. The ice from last night's frost has not yet melted in the birdbath. The blackbird has visited it several times, has looked at the ice then flown away.'

I heard her gasp, as if someone had struck her in the face. 'Harry died an hour ago,' she said. 'He asked me to call you.' She began to sob and was unable to go on. I murmured my helpless, comfortless words to her. When she had regained a little control she apologised and said, 'At the end he smiled and closed his eyes, and he gripped my hand in his and said in such a clear ringing voice, *There is no pain, there is no pain.* And then he left me.'

After Christine's call I stood at the window and looked out into my wintry garden. The naked branches of the apple tree were black against the cold grey sky. I said aloud to the silence, 'Oh, my dear little Harry!' and I wept. And as I wept for the death of the brother I had so seldom seen during his life, I was remembering his birth. My two sisters and I waiting in the front room of our flat, crouched together by the dying embers of the coal fire, I in my pyjamas and the girls in their nightdresses. We gazed into the embers of the fire, seeing those scenes of the imagination that inspire our fears and uncertainties when we are children. I have no memory of my mother crying out, only that my father alone acted as the midwife of the occasion. It seemed to have come upon us suddenly. I had hardly known my mother to be expecting another child; I had thought we five were our entire family. My father came out of our parents' bedroom and he stood over us and we looked up at him in great anxiety and perplexity. His sleeves were rolled above his elbows, his collarless shirt open at his neck, his bare chest gleaming in the firelight with beads of sweat, the great white and purple scars of his wound deforming his arm. As he stood looking down at us I saw a gentleness in my father's gaze that was strange and distant. I had never seen such a look in my father's eyes before. He was like a stranger. Another man. I gazed with faint horror at the livid and disfiguring scars of his wound. He smiled and said to us softly, 'Come in and kiss your wee brother.'

In the half-light of our parents' bedroom my mother lay with the tiny baby in her arms, cradling it to her breast. As our father instructed, we each leaned over in turn and kissed our new brother on his forehead. My lips trembled as they touched the magical translucence of his skin, so tender the lightest blow would surely dissolve him. Was he as yet quite with us, I wondered, or was he the advance of himself—a promise of what the world might be, of what we humans might be before we are born, an image of unsettling perfection? Precious beyond reckoning by the ordinary values of our days, he was my brother: a gift I had not expected to receive. I looked my questions into my mother's beautiful dark eyes, and she smiled and looked down at him, her new son.

After we had left the bedroom, my father mixed a bucket of wet dross and built the smoking hummock behind the glowing coals in the grate, then he sat in his armchair and lit his straight-stemmed pipe, tamping the tobacco in the bowl with his thumb, the nail of which was broken and discoloured. We three waited for him, sitting silently on the hearthrug watching as he got his pipe going. He tossed a final match into the fire and said, 'Your mother and I are calling him after my brother, your uncle Harry.' We had never met our uncle Harry, nor, I believe, had I ever before heard him referred to.

My young brother, Harry was the last surviving member of my childhood family, that other home and family long before Jo and I met. That night, as I lay sleepless in my bed, listening to the cold taking possession of the house, I felt myself to be truly alone at last. Was it not the true condition I had sought for myself ever since the day I left home as a boy of sixteen, my loving parents weeping and baffled by my decision, they and my brother and two sisters a sorrowing group on the platform at Liverpool Street Station? My motives were unknown to me then. Why did I leave all that was dear and familiar to me for a wilderness on the furthest side of the world? To find a desert where I could no longer be reached. It was an act as strangely idealistic in its way as my brother's passion for classical music. I lost contact. I ceased to exist for those I had left behind.

I rose from bed and once more stood at the small six-paned cottage window and gazed out across the moonlit lawn at the apple tree, knowing myself to be quite alone at last.

Before the apples are ripe each year, a flock of small, brightly coloured birds appears as if from nowhere, called by some mysterious signal, and begins to feast noisily on the small green apples, a throng of them feasting, a happy annual celebration of abundance. The daily visits of these small birds are a delight, and when one day they cease to come, as suddenly and inexplicably as they first arrive, the garden seems to be deserted and silent.

I went to my study and emailed my daughter, Hennie, who lives in Bordeaux. Her decision to live on the other side of the world mirrored my own youthful decision to leave the place of my origin behind. I suggested she visit me here. It had been some years since my last visit to her in Europe and I felt the need to see her. As a little girl she and I were especially close.

THE DEAL

* * *

After my brother's death, the image of my father sitting under an apple tree in an orchard somewhere in Europe towards the close of the Second World War began to haunt me. So vivid was this scene in my imagination that it was as if my brother had left with me a snapshot. This half-imaginary, half-real scene called to me so strongly and so persistently that I found it difficult to explain and began to think that my dead brother was somehow influencing my thoughts and that he wanted me, the family's storyteller, to meditate on the significance of this image of our father's wounding. I remembered the time in our living room in the flat when my father received his campaign medals. For several minutes he sat mutely staring at them in his lap, then he suddenly snatched them up, rose from his chair and went out to the toilet. We heard him flush it several times. His contempt for the establishment has stayed with me all my life. After Christine's call, I began to feel my brother's urging so strongly that I ceased to be able to keep my mind on my work and, instead of working, I would sit for hours thinking about it, the work forgotten on the desk before me.

My father's wounding and his angry rejection of his medals were so far away in the past they might as well have been from another world entirely. It did not seem possible to me then that

I would be able to find my way to the origins of those scenes with my father, or to their meaning for me, from where I stood in the present, now an old man myself, older by some years than he had been when he passed away. I had listened again and again to the andante movement of that Mozart sonata, and each time I listened I heard in it my brother's voice, filled with joy, goodwill and sound, practical common sense. And as I listened the music was accompanied by the scene I had not witnessed but had only imagined of my father sitting under an apple tree the instant before he was struck down and his life, and the lives of his children and his wife, changed forever. The apple tree he sat under eventually became the apple tree in my garden that I could see from the window in my sitting room and which I often gazed at while the music was playing.

In this scene my father inhabited for me the moment before the apocalypse, as in Yeats's poem, in which things are changed, changed utterly, and a terrible beauty is born. Why, I asked myself, had my brother said, *Our father* received *his wound while sitting under an apple tree* and not used the more usual construction, *Our father* was wounded *while sitting under an apple tree?*

He *received* his wound, my brother said, as if he were saying our father received his stigmata, the sign of the cross he would bear for the rest of his life. One receives grace. One receives something sacred that is bestowed upon one, or which is conferred in a ceremonial way, a distinction, or some reward of office or acknowledgement. Priests, my dictionary reminds me, receive confession. Does one also receive a wound in such a way? The wound that life reserves for each of us? Is that, in the end, the point of it?

In a way that I could not then explain, I also knew that my brother's death had fixed in my mind the image of my father's wounding, as if there were, in that other violent moment, a key that would enable me to deal with my grief and my failure to become the artist my father had hoped I would be, becoming instead a writer of imaginary worlds.

When I at last gave in to the urging of the image of my wounded father, the very first thought I recorded in my diary that day was: *My father would disapprove of this*. My thoughts, I remember, were touched on that occasion by feelings of guilt at the knowledge that I was about to trespass upon a part of my father's life about which he had remained silent. My father had been dead for almost thirty years already when I made this note, and yet I made the note in the present tense, as if I believed my father to be still capable of demonstrating disapproval. Which of course he was, if I am to acknowledge his influence on the formation of my own conscience. It was his disapproval that haunted me when I took part in the deal. The unspoken compact he and I had made was sullied by my decision to help my friend. I look back now and I ask myself once again if Lang was truly the friend I then thought him to be.

I had in my hand a photograph of me and my father when I was no more than five or six years of age. I am lying across my father's raised legs, his bare feet against my stomach, my arms outstretched, my legs together behind me, my toes pointed. I am being not a cross but an aeroplane. With my father's help I am flying. It is on his strength and on his magical ability to believe, an ability I hope to possess myself when I am grown up and have come into a full inheritance of my adult emotions and the gifts of spirit that he will bequeath to me; it is in this, in my father's faith in my ability to fly one day, that I placed my trust. It is a good photograph. Indeed, it is a photograph of goodness. There is no hint of distress or uncertainty between the father and his son; it shows only the happiness of the father and the happiness of his young son on a summer day in the English countryside. Their joy and their delight at being together. They are sharing their dream of flying. The war, if such a thing can exist in the same world as happiness, is so far away from their thoughts that it does not exist for them in that moment.

An old man now, I hold the photograph under the light and look more closely at it, and I wonder who it was that stood behind the lens and stole this little scene from time. Was it my mother or was it, perhaps, my sister? Neither my father nor I am aware of the photographer or of her camera. It is that kind of enviable snapshot which lacks the stiffness of pose or composition and which has captured a moment of life *as it is lived*, without a consciousness of the passing of time. The subjects, my father and I, are oblivious of time and of everything but ourselves.

I turn the photograph over to see if perhaps there is something written on the back. But there is nothing, just the brownish spots of foxing, the first visible signs of decay. Where was the photograph taken? We are in the country. In a field beside a hedge. In England in those days it was still possible to tell where in the country one was by the style of the hedge. This is a hedge on a bank of earth and the hedge itself is principally of layered hawthorns. The hawthorns have been allowed to grow out for a season or two, and the hedge is looking wild and neglected, which is no doubt due to the shortage of farm labour during the war and the pressure of other, more necessary tasks in the attempt to make England self-reliant in the production of food. So we are somewhere in the west of England. Not so far west as to be in the country of beech hedges, but further west than the upright hedges of hazel and blackberry more to the east, where the hedges are not grown on banks of earth as they are in the west.

The photograph of myself and my father brought to my mind the memory of being in a car for the first time. There was the excitement of looking out at the streets and people going by as if we were no longer part of that world. And then the bleak cold smell of the Lodge, only it wasn't called the Lodge but something else. Being left there. Abandoned by my father to the cold hand of the white-clad nurse, the keeper of the children, preventing me from following my father out the door into the bright street again. The feeling of being lost to love and the family. A feeling that never quite left me but became a small dark evil—a word I would rarely have cause to use. An evil world in that children's home, as it was called, though there was nothing of home or hearth or welcome about it but only the cold hard-knuckled hand of the big woman. It was there I received my wound.

Arranging memories, like sorting old letters and photographs that have been shoved in a drawer or a shoebox for years and forgotten, putting them into the order of their dates, some of the date stamps difficult to decipher as they always are, so having to take the letter out of its envelope to read it for an idea of where in the pile it might find its place. Hoping to make a pattern out of the random loot of time past. And getting involved in the letter and remembering receiving it and the feeling it gave one to hear this or that piece of news, such as my mother getting my father to set up the new bird feeder on the little square of grass outside the back window when she was old, so that she could sit inside in the warm with a cup of tea and a digestive biscuit, a novel open in her lap, and watch the sparrows come and feed and sometimes see a couple of starlings chasing them off, or the blackbird, which she did not mind. Arranging such memories. The leavings of the past, turning over what I found there, looking for sparkling little gems and signs of colour and connections but finding mostly a damp grey dross, heavy and unwilling to take the fire of imagination. Under my gaze, the world of my old people dissolving and disappearing, disintegrating into dust and blowing away when it feels the touch of the day. Nothing of note to be salvaged intact. Glimpses only. Little flashes of this and that, to begin with. The war. I wanted to write it in capital letters: *THE WAR.* How would I ever find him now? Wasn't it too late?

THE DEAL

THE DEAL

3

1975. Andy is thirty-nine.

It was not until Andy McPherson's second term teaching English part-time at the school that he met the art master, Lang Tzu. When Andy entered the staffroom and saw Lang standing on his own smoking a cigarette, he went straight up to him and introduced himself. The impression he had of Lang was of a small, wiry-looking man of around fifty. He was wearing pale slacks and a short-sleeved shirt of some light material. The staffroom was chilly but Lang did not seem bothered by this. He was a man who must once have been handsome. He had about him the look of a thoughtful person who stands alone by choice, almost as if to stand alone was his destiny. Andy imagined him to be a Han Chinese with an aristocratic past. He was attracted to him at once and began to create a romantic story around his presence at the school. He wasn't surprised when Lang responded to his greeting politely but with a quiet kind of pleasure. After a brief exchange, Lang suggested they go to the pub during the lunch break.

The pub was a small family concern on a corner of one of the back streets behind the school, a relic hanging on from the days when there had been a thriving drinking hole on nearly every corner. Dom, the barman, was also the licensee. He greeted Lang by his given name. Andy felt at home with the smell of cigarettes and stale beer; it reminded him of backstreet bars in London he had visited with his father, places where his father was greeted as Jock by the barmen. To Andy as a boy, the smell was of the grown-up world of men, something of mystery and danger in it.

There were no other customers in the pub. Dom, a large florid man in his sixties, pulled a beer for Andy then poured a glass of red wine from an open bottle and set it in front of Lang. Lang sculled the contents of the glass and Dom refilled it, leaving the wine bottle in front of Lang before returning to sit on a stool behind the bar, down at the far end. There he poured himself a double shot of Scotch and resumed studying the form guide, making notes in the margins of the newspaper with a pencil, which he wet with the tip of his tongue every few minutes. The races were playing on a small television that sat with bottles of spirits on the shelf beside him. Sausage rolls and half-a-dozen pies rested on a glass shelf in an electric warmer at the end of the bar, a bottle of tomato sauce and a pile of paper serviettes beside it. Every now and then Dom looked up from the form guide and took off his glasses and squinted at the television screen.

Standing at the bar that first day of their meeting, it seemed to Andy there was a natural ease between himself and Lang, and he began to imagine a grand friendship. Why not? He had heard of such friendships. Didn't all men long to enjoy that special connection with another man? A precious brotherhood, wasn't it?

They told each other something of their lives, and at one point Lang said, 'What do you do?'

Andy laughed. 'Well, I'm teaching part-time at the school, aren't I?'

'But what do you really do?' Lang was serious and wanted to hear something substantial from Andy, to confirm something for himself, perhaps to settle a doubt.

Andy said, 'I'm an unpublished writer.'

Lang seemed delighted by this. 'And I'm a failed artist.' The admission amused him. 'I was once an artist, so of course I failed.' He lifted his glass of wine and drank.

Andy watched him refill the glass from the bottle. 'What do you mean, of course you failed? Why of course?'

'Art is a striving after something beyond our reach. So we always fail. Art is our dream. It is our longing for something that can never be ours. I abandoned art, but she refused to abandon me.' He laughed. It was not a big open laugh but a small inward chuckle, gazing down into his wine and sharing the idea with himself, suggesting more was going on in his mind than he was open to revealing. He looked up and smiled at Andy. 'It's not so easy to escape from art once you've embraced her. She's like a woman in love with you. She hangs on to you and in the end you give up struggling to free yourself from her and accept her presence as your destiny.' He studied Andy closely for a moment, as if he might still be unsure. 'I became a collector. And an adviser to those who can know nothing of art: men and women who are unable to dream and know only how to own things.'

'And you are contemptuous of them?'

'Oh no! I feel no contempt.'

'But you're still really an artist?' Andy was thinking of his father when his father came home after the war, bewildered and wounded in his body and his soul, a man changed and humiliated by the horrors, a man barely hanging on to his humanity. It was years before he did it, but he did eventually take up his brushes and begin to paint again, puzzled and searching all the while for his lost self. Andy believed his father's way back from the dead had been through art. And so Andy became a believer in the redemptive power of art. The relief in the home the day his father took out his painting things and began again to be the father and husband he had once been. And there was the new son, Harry, for whom redemption came to lie within the private world of music.

'Artists don't have a choice,' Lang said. 'We don't decide. Art decides for us. I was born in Hangzhou. I spent the first ten years of my life in that lost world with my mother and her father, before my own father, who was a wealthy Shanghai merchant, sent me to Australia to board at a school in Ballarat, where we had relatives. As soon as I arrived in Ballarat, I knew I had to become an Australian and I abandoned everything Chinese to achieve that end.' He laughed and looked at Andy. 'I didn't know then that a Chinese could never be an Aussie bloke.'

Lang spoke of his origins as if he thought it had all been a great joke, a trick that had diverted him from his true course. But beneath his surface candour Andy sensed in Lang a melancholy that was deep and elusive, which he found moving and wonderfully attractive. Standing there, observing Lang leaning on the scarred edge of the bar beside him, the slim fingers of his hand clasping his wineglass, his narrow shoulders rounded, a small, sensitive, vulnerable man, Andy felt deeply drawn to him.

Lang said, 'What do you write?'

'Unreadable and unfinished novels.'

Lang gazed into his empty wineglass.

Andy said, 'Three of them.'

Lang looked up sideways at him.

They both laughed.

Lang lifted his glass. 'Here's to your unpublished novels.'

Andy caught the eye of Dom, who was nursing his whisky. Dom too lifted his glass. 'Here's to you, mate.'

'Thanks.' Andy drained his glass.

They hurried back to the school, Lang hunched against the chill breeze, protected only by his short-sleeved cotton shirt. Before they parted, Lang suggested Andy might come out to his house one evening soon to view his collection of paintings.

4

Two years before he started teaching part-time at the technical school and met Lang Tzu, Andy had met Jo on a night bus to Sydney. As he was making his way along the aisle looking for a seat, Jo gave him a smile. Encouraged by her welcoming smile, he sat in the spare seat next to her. 'Hi, I'm Andy.'

'Jo,' she said. 'It's short for Josephine.'

When he was settled, he turned to her. 'Where are you going?'

She laughed. 'We're on the bus to Sydney, aren't we?'

'It stops at other places along the way, though, doesn't it? You might have been going to Wagga.'

'Well, I'm not,' she said. 'I'm going to see my aunt Henrietta. She lives in Double Bay. Aren't you going all the way to Sydney?'

'I am—right through to Central Station.' He looked at the book she had lying facedown in her lap, her left hand partly concealing it, the orange cover of the Penguin standing out against the pale green of her jeans. She was wearing some kind of Indian cotton top with an intricate pattern and a low square-cut neck. Her hair was short and dark and glossy. She looked to be in her mid-twenties. He said, 'What are you reading?'

She glanced down at the book. 'Simone de Beauvoir. It's a novel. *The Mandarins*.'

'How's it going?'

'It's not as good as her non-fiction. I don't think she's really a novelist.'

'I've never read her.' He wondered what Jo meant by Beauvoir not really being a novelist. Was he really a novelist himself? Was there some quality that distinguished novelists from everyone else? He was about to ask her what she meant when the bus pulled out into the evening traffic, the last of the daylight glancing off the high city buildings.

Jo said, 'So why are you going to Sydney?'

'Just to look around. Check out the galleries and the library. The bus was cheaper than the train. Are you staying with your aunt?'

'No, she's gone into palliative care. I'll stay in her house in Double Bay. I've stayed there often. Ever since I was little.'

He tried to imagine her being little.

'What's that for?' she said.

'What?'

'That funny little smile.'

'I was imagining you being little.'

They gazed into each other's eyes for a long time. Jo broke the spell by putting her hand in his. Her confident touch flooded through Andy's body like a hit from a drug. Her presence beside him was making him dizzy. He took a couple of deep breaths to steady himself. He had to tell her. 'I'm too old for you, Jo.'

She laughed. 'Bullshit!'

'I'm thirty-seven.'

She gripped his hand firmly and looked into his eyes. 'Don't let go!' She spoke in a tone that warned him not to argue.

He couldn't help grinning. 'You mean it!'

'I'm glad you understand.'

They held hands all the way and later she slept against his shoulder. Andy couldn't sleep. He looked out of the window at the lonely lights of farmsteads off in the darkness, Jo's head resting against him. When she woke, he said, 'You smell like my home.' Her cheek was flushed where she'd been leaning against him. He was sure he had known her forever. In some other, more perfect, life. A life of childhood where dreams come true. He was afraid she must wake up from the spell and know then the truth, that he really was too old for her.

She fluffed her hair and straightened her jacket and tucked in her blouse and she clambered over him to go to the toilet. He waited for her to return. In the early morning light, the tyres of the bus hummed on the Hume Highway.

She came back drying her hands on her jeans. She pulled down her backpack from the overhead storage and shared with him the food she had brought for the journey. Tomato-and-lettuce sandwiches that had gone soft, a slice of seedcake that still smelled of the oven, and sweet black tea from her thermos. They took turns sipping the hot tea from the thermos lid, which they used as a cup. She asked him where he was going to be staying in Sydney. He said he didn't know yet. After a few minutes she said, 'Stay with me at Aunt Henrietta's.'

It was sunny and there was a small garden out the front of the care home. He sat on a bench and waited for Jo. When she came out he saw that she had been crying. She sat next to him and didn't speak for a while. He said nothing. A black-headed ibis was raiding the rubbish bin out on the footpath.

Jo said, 'There's nothing I can do for her. She's in a coma.' She sat looking at Andy for a while.

He took her hand. 'What are you thinking?'

'I was thinking what a strange thing it is that Aunt Hennie should be dying just as you come into my life. She's the only family I've got. Now I have you.' She leaned in and they kissed. It was a long kiss into which they put all their feelings.

'I've known you forever,' he said.

'Yes, I know,' she said.

They stayed there sitting side by side on the garden seat out the front of the home for a long time, holding hands and leaning against each other and not saying much: Andy watching the ibis, with which he had made a connection; Jo seeing her aunt, whom she had loved since she was a child.

Over the following few days, Jo visited the home every morning to sit with her dying aunt, and Andy waited for her outside on the bench. The ibis was always there, fossicking in the bin. Sometimes it was joined by another ibis. It was hard to tell which was the original ibis and which was the newcomer. Impossible really. Andy said to them, 'You're just ibis.' They ignored him, as they ignored the occasional passer-by.

After their morning visit to the care home, Jo showed Sydney to Andy. They sat outside a cafe on Circular Quay and drank coffee and ate croissants and told each other about their lives. They laughed a lot. For some reason even the bad things in their past seemed funny. Jo was twenty-seven and had an economics degree. She had a job cataloguing interesting old books for an antiquarian book dealer in Melbourne. 'The pay's not great but I love the people and the job.'

Andy told her about his life in the bush before writing and then doing a degree in literature and history. 'I'm never going to have a career in a serious profession,' he said. 'I may never make any money writing. It's a gamble, but I have to do it. I don't know why.'

'I knew you were like that the second I saw you looking for a seat on the bus,' Jo said. 'A voice in my head said to me, *Here he comes, Josephine! Don't fuck this up!*'

And they laughed at this too. Everything was funny.

At night they made love in Aunt Hennie's guest bedroom in the big soft bed in her beautiful old cottage where she had lived alone for her last years, and first thing each morning they went out into her small back garden and picked fresh leaves and flowers so the place would stay fresh and alive.

They could not keep away from each other even for a moment. The magnetic force keeping them together was so strong it exhausted them. But still they held hands and laughed and made love and looked into each other's eyes and said with astonishment things like, 'Can this really be real?' And, 'How have I managed to live for so long without you?' And slowly they began to believe it. Slowly, during that week in Sydney, it began to become their reality.

THE DEAL

* * *

On Wednesday afternoon Jo took him to Bronte Beach for a swim. He had to buy a pair of togs first. They were sitting on the sand after they came out of the water, the sun was shining, and the day was warm and still, the waves rolling in and breaking monotonously, rolling up the sand, then retreating and breaking again. There were a few people in, swimming, bodysurfing. But mostly people were lying around in the sun getting tanned, reading books or with their eyes closed, or dabbing their skin with tanning lotion. Most were with someone, a friend or a partner, but a few were on their own. There were hardly any children and only one old person. It was the middle of a normal working day, and no doubt the children were at school. Andy wondered how these people lying around in the sun could afford to do it. Didn't they have jobs to go to?

Jo was at home in the water. She took Andy into the surf where he was tumbled around in the waves. She laughed at his fear of sharks. Afterwards they sat wrapped in their towels and Jo told Andy about her family. Jo's parents had split up and divorced after her father had an affair with her mother's best friend. Jo was seven at the time. She had gone to live with Aunt Hennie and eventually lost touch with her parents. Andy thought of his own mother and father. He had always taken it for granted that they were loyal to each other. He still believed that to have been the case. It was a kind of sacred truth for him. He wondered how Jo could feel so free to tell him about these intimate failures of her family. If he had known something like that about his own parents, he was sure he would not have told Jo but would have kept it to himself.

Like Andy's brother, Harry, Jo had been a late child. She had no sisters or brothers.

When they got back to Melbourne after Aunt Henrietta's funeral, Andy left the room he had been renting in a big old Victorian house full of single working men in Port Melbourne, and he and Jo rented a one-bedroom flat in South Yarra. They had no furniture, just a mattress. Andy woke up one night and saw that Jo was crying. When he asked her what was wrong she said, 'Nothing's wrong, idiot! I want a baby.'

When Andy heard this it was as if a tap was turned on inside him, releasing a lovely warm feeling of a kind he had never experienced before. 'Well then, let's have a baby.' And Jo laughed through her tears and they made love.

Afterwards, lying there in each other's arms, Jo said, 'I want to have *our* baby. Ours. I've never wanted a baby with anyone else.'

Andy wondered how many others there had been. He felt fiercely jealous and wanted to ask Jo if she was still in touch with any of them. But he kept these thoughts to himself and said, 'I've never given children a thought before. I've always imagined I would never be a father.'

'And now do you want to be a father?' There was just a touch of anxiety in this question.

'I can't think of anything more wonderful than you having our baby. I'll have to take my life more seriously.'

5

By spring the following year Jo was pregnant. She was going into the antiquarian bookshop every day during the week, while Andy was back at his part-time job as a storeman in a wholesale electrical fittings warehouse in Port Melbourne. Jo said he should use his degree to get a job teaching; the pay was better, and there were the holidays. Andy was resisting the idea. Some of his fellow students at the university had gone into teaching. He had always felt that if he were to become a teacher it would be falling into line, admitting to himself that he was just another standard clone with an arts degree. He thought of teaching as a kind of baseline that he would never submit to.

THE DEAL

Then one day Jo received a cheque in the mail for fifty-seven thousand dollars. The cheque was from Aunt Henrietta's old lawyer, who had also been the executor of her will. When Andy got home from work Jo handed him the cheque. They stood together in the narrow space of their kitchen in the rented flat and looked at it. 'We're blessed,' she said, and she put her arm through his. She was moved. 'I'll never feel as if this is really ours.' She was thinking of when she was a child staying with her aunt in Sydney, and then the final moment. Hennie lying there under a light blanket alone in a cold room, the blind over the window screening the purity of the day outside. Lying on her back, her hands by her sides outside the covering, dressed in a freshly ironed cotton nightie, the top button done up, as if she had been a nun. The nurse told Jo her aunt had finally passed, as she put it, and left her alone to say her goodbye.

Alone with her aunt in that barren room, she had crouched beside the bed and taken Hennie's bony hand in her own and told Hennie how much she loved her and that she would miss her forever. Hennie's hand had contracted, Jo was sure of it, as if Hennie was responding from the depths of her death coma, way out in the dark, far beyond recall, the love still giving life to her corpse. The nurse later dismissed the contraction of Hennie's hand. 'You must have imagined it. We don't move after we're dead.' But Jo believed Hennie could hear her and was communicating to her the last moments of their love, the secret power of love that briefly defeats the empty silence of death. But then, Jo believed all the most important things were a mystery, things like love and the strangeness of communications between people. The way, for example, she and Andy had known the moment they saw each other on the bus that they were meant for each other, for life. How could they have known? But they did know. And she didn't care that he was ten years older than her. 'Our souls are the same age,' she had said to him when he asked her about this.

Fifty-seven thousand dollars. Andy had never seen such a large amount of money before. He didn't know what to say. He was feeling a certain amount of confusion. He'd taken care of himself since he left home, and he disliked the feeling now of benefiting from the will of Jo's old aunt, a woman he had never met. He said finally, 'This much money will trivialise our struggles.' There he was, talking about struggle and impossible dreams again. With a baby on the way he was going to have to provide Jo and the child with something more substantial than struggle and dreams. With money and a child, life was no longer going to be so romantic.

Jo said, 'We're going to be a family.' She flapped the cheque at him. 'This is our house!'

He thought of a poem by Rilke whose sentiments he had identified with before he met Jo. *Whoever has no house now, will never have one./ Whoever is alone will stay alone.* His solitary dreaming days were over; that version of himself as a lone figure with no place of his own, an image he'd treasured, as if he were some kind of free travelling scholar in a medieval landscape of the mind, a figure on the margins seeking some kind of special meaning that would set him apart from everyone else, was no longer appropriate to his reality. So far he had produced nothing with which to support the view of himself as someone apart and special. The three unpublished novels had been abandoned. He had known they were no good. Had known they were something he could never be proud of. After his initial anger at having his work repeatedly rejected, he had eventually come to accept that there must be something essentially wrong with these novels, but he didn't know what that was and the publishers who rejected them did not tell him. His failure puzzled and disappointed him at first, and at times he had felt helpless. But he had never thought of giving up. He knew instinctively that success lay in surviving the torments of failure. Others had done it. And he could do it. If he were to give up his dream, then he really would be lost, even with Jo beside him. There was, after all, surely a limit to the power of love and intimacy to sustain meaning in his life.

They went to the local pub for a beer and dinner the evening of Hennie's cheque, and talked about Jo's ideal house. On the weekend they went looking for it. Each weekend from then on they spent looking for the house Jo had in her mind, the house that was to be their home. They soon realised they needed a car. They bought a second-hand Holden station wagon from a dealer in Elizabeth Street. It was white and had a couple of dents in the panel work that had been crudely repaired. Andy asked the salesman if it had been in an accident. The salesman patted the bonnet and said confidently, 'No, sir. This little beauty is as clean as the day she came off the production line.'

Jo gave the salesman a cheque from the account they'd put Aunt Henrietta's money in and Andy drove the car home and parked it beside the flats in the spot allocated to them. It was the first car either of them had ever owned but not the first Andy had ever driven. On the cattle station in Queensland where he had worked before coming down south to the university, he had driven many different vehicles, including the boss's new Ford Customline and a left-hand-drive ex-US army jeep, as well as an ancient Fargo prime mover with a tray for carrying fence posts and other bulky materials. His Queensland driver's licence had been issued to him free for ten years and was still current.

They didn't use the station wagon for getting to work but left it parked outside their flat and took the tram. The car was for weekends and the search for Jo's ideal home, which they would buy with Aunt Hennie's money.

THE DEAL

* * *

Their first weekend with the car they found the house Jo was dreaming of, but it was seventy thousand dollars. The agent said they should take out a small mortgage and buy it at once, as such houses rarely came onto the market and were usually priced around eighty to a hundred thousand. 'This one is a bargain and a great opportunity for you to get into the property market. I shouldn't tell you this, but the owners are splitting up and need a quick sale. Your deposit today will secure this house for you and your family into the future.'

Jo and Andy looked at each other. Jo wanted the house. 'We can be a family here,' she said to Andy, her dream in her eyes. She might already have been at home, standing there in that house with its view over a lovely garden with fruit trees and flowerbeds and a lawn. They were in the kitchen, which had been extended into the back garden to form a sunroom. And the sun was shining and the kitchen appliances were all new and of the latest model. The house itself was in a row of double-storey brick Victorian houses in a terrace in South Melbourne. There was a small park across the road. It was perfect, really, except for the price, which put it tantalisingly out of their reach. Jo was tempted. Andy said, 'Going into debt is too easy.'

Jo, who was the one doing the talking, as it was really her money she was talking about, told the estate agent they would need to think about it. She was hoping to convince Andy. They went to a cafe on Clarendon Street and sat in the only free booth. The place was cheerful and full of the chatter and laughter of the other customers. They ordered coffee and a salad sandwich then held hands and looked at each other.

Jo said, 'What do you think? This is such a nice area to live in.' She was imagining them in the house.

Andy said, 'My mum and dad never borrowed money. Not even buying things on time payment. If Mum needed something, they saved up for it.' The thought of owing thousands of dollars and having to think about repaying it made him uneasy. 'If we borrow that money, we won't belong to ourselves; we'll belong to them. We'll lose our freedom. We should keep looking till we find a house we can afford.'

Jo withdrew her hand from his. It was the first time they had come to an impasse of this kind. She picked up her sandwich and took a bite and sat chewing, saying nothing. The view of the street through the windows reminded her of a French Impressionist painting. She said, 'Sitting here we could be in Paris.'

Andy said, 'It's always going to be that our ideal house, and our ideal anything else, will be just out of our reach. That's the way it is. That's life. If we lean too far over, we'll fall in the shit and never get ourselves out again.' He took a big bite out of his salad sandwich and chewed for a while. Then he said,

'If we borrow that money I'll end up working full-time to pay it off instead of writing.'

Jo looked at him. 'That's your real reason?'

'Yes, it is.'

She left it at that. Andy seemed hard suddenly. Implacable. She hadn't seen this side of him before and she didn't like it.

The following weekend he said they should be looking at houses in the Port, which was an old part of the city and a lot cheaper owing to the factories and industrial sites, like the big rubber factory where most of the Greek migrants worked. They soon saw a house for sale that fitted the bill. They called in at the real estate agent and the young woman who was handling the sale took them back to the house for a look. 'It's empty now. It's had tenants in it for years.'

The house was a large two-storey Victorian with party walls each side but not exactly a terrace. The neighbouring houses were single-storey. Jo and Andy and the agent stood out the front looking at it.

Jo said, 'I don't think I could live down here. It's all so ugly. This whole area.' There was too much traffic and she didn't like the dingy-looking Housing Commission flats opposite. And one of the panes in the front window of the house was broken, the gap covered with a piece of weathered and warped three-ply. 'It looks dilapidated,' she said.

'I couldn't live here.' She could be implacable too. After all, it was Aunt Hennie's money and she could decide what to do with it. It was anger and disappointment that were making her think like this. Was this where they would bring up their child? She couldn't see it.

Coming into Hennie's money had seemed to divide her and Andy. She could sense him growing closed off and determined, and she was beginning to feel like that herself. The purity of being in love, the wonderful simplicity of it, had melted away and been replaced by this calculating kind of mood between them. She tried to recall how they'd been on the bus to Sydney, but she couldn't. She would rather have given the money away and forgotten about the house altogether if it was going to destroy their joy in being with each other. But the baby inside her was real and would need a proper home. She was confused, conflicted in her thinking, and downhearted as they stood there in front of this neglected old house, the traffic roaring past a few feet away, the air stinking with diesel fumes.

Andy had grown up on a housing estate in South London and the flats didn't trouble him. He knew they were occupied by people like his own family. Just ordinary people. The road, however, was an over-dimensional route leading from the port to the eastern suburbs, was choked with trucks and commercial vehicles, as well as private cars heading out of or into the Port and the city centre. And, as Jo said, it was *down here*, at the bottom of the hill and at the bottom, or just beyond the bottom, of the area where professional people would choose to live and bring up their children.

The agent said straight out to Jo, 'I don't blame you for hesitating. It's been on the market for two years. He's asking seventy, but I know he'll accept almost any offer. He's gone back to live in Greece—on Rhodes, lucky bastard. He's overextended here and the bank will soon be calling in their loan.' She looked Jo in the eye. 'It's an amazing opportunity to acquire a magnificent piece of inner Melbourne property. There's a private garden out the back. Come and have a look.'

They didn't catch what she said next over the roar of the traffic accelerating when the lights changed. She unlocked the front door and stepped aside for them to enter.

Andy thanked her and said to Jo, 'Just have a look.' He had to raise his voice to make himself heard. She wasn't exactly sulky, but Andy thought she was being difficult. Was she going to be like this whenever she didn't get what she wanted? Aunt Henrietta's favourite little girl? Spoiled, his mother would have said, passing a swift judgement. He took her hand and gave it a squeeze.

They went in ahead of the agent and stood in the dark passage. The air smelled of damp. The agent closed the heavy timber door behind her. The moment the door closed there was silence. The roar of the traffic was distant. A calm descended.

Andy said, 'Jesus! It's a fortress.' He decided the house had a good feeling about it.

The front room had an open fireplace. They looked in then went on down the passage. The staircase had been painted white. Andy said, 'I bet you this is Australian cedar underneath this paint.'

Jo stood and looked and said nothing.

The agent led them up the stairs, Andy following her and Jo reluctantly bringing up the rear. There was a landing halfway up the stairs, a large window shedding sunlight onto the worn carpet. A diagonal crack in the lower pane of the window. At the top of the stairs they turned left into a large room facing the street. They went in and looked. A ceiling rose and an open fireplace suggested a once-prosperous past. The agent said, 'Great potential here for a lovely sitting room or a master bedroom. And you can always enclose the balcony with windows. It will catch the sun in the winter.'

Andy said, 'It could be really great.'

Jo said nothing.

They traipsed out of the room, the agent in the lead. A funeral party.

On the other side of the landing there were two large bedrooms; the further one, overlooking roofs and back lanes, was reached by passing through the first bedroom. The walls of both rooms were papered with red-and-black-patterned wallpaper. The central lampshade in the larger of the two rooms was a scarlet half-globe with golden tassels. Jo laughed. 'It looks like this must have been a brothel.'

They went downstairs and through a room with an open fireplace. The proportions of this central room were impressive, with the high ceiling and elaborate fire surrounds. A window looked out onto an enclosed square area, with a small tiled bathroom leading off it, a shower over the old enamel bath, a smell of damp and decay. Beyond the bathroom square was a long narrow room with a window onto a side lane, sunlight falling onto the timber floor and reflecting off the grey walls. A sudden bright cheerfulness. They went on through this room to an old-fashioned kitchen, a massive crack in the right-hand brick wall. Andy looked through onto the concreted yard and barbecue area next door.

The agent opened the kitchen door into the backyard. 'Come and have a look.'

They stepped out into a sunny patch of rubble and broken concrete, thistles and weedy grasses growing up through the cracks. A pale rose clambering over an outhouse was flowering, its double blooms perfuming the air.

Jo went over to the rose and sniffed. She turned to Andy, excited. 'It's Félicité et Perpétue—Aunt Hennie's favourite rose! It's the one growing over the front gate at her cottage. Remember?'

The sun shone on the rose. The sound of the heavy traffic on the over-dimensional route was a long way off, and the ugly flats opposite were out of sight and forgotten.

The agent glanced at Andy, one eyebrow raised, then stepped across the narrow yard to stand beside Jo. She leaned in and sniffed the rose. 'What a gorgeous perfume!'

The two women smiled at each other, the white rose blossoms held between them.

Andy thought how beautiful Jo looked, smiling and holding the rose, standing there in the sunlight, happy. The thought slipped into his mind: *Thank you, Aunt Hennie!* And he found that he too was smiling. He said, 'We can soon turn this junkyard into a beautiful private haven where our child can play.'

'Children!' Jo said, laughing.

6

Their daughter, Henrietta, was born at five o'clock on the morning of Wednesday, 7 May 1975, at the Freemasons Maternity Hospital. Despite the impressive amount of blood, the doctor described it as an easy birth. Andy was a nervous onlooker at the event. When he heard the doctor's steel shears slicing Jo's sensitive flesh to ease the opening, his knees went weak.

In her bed afterwards in the ward, the bright red baby swaddled and tucked in against her breast, Jo smiled at Andy and denied that it had been painful. She was emotional and said she loved him and she shed a few tears. She released a hand from the bedclothes and took his hand in hers. 'Isn't she the most beautiful baby you've ever seen?'

He agreed. 'Of course she is.' The truth was, he had only ever seen one other baby as new as this in his entire life. He leaned down and kissed his tiny daughter on top of her bald head and he breathed her delicate smell. When his lips touched her, he had a sudden vivid memory of kissing his newborn brother after his father delivered him in his parents' bedroom.

In what felt like no time at all they were living in the Port Melbourne house. Andy spent every minute of his spare time clearing the backyard of concrete and rubble and barrowing it along the side lane to the dump bin he'd hired. The neighbours were taking the opportunity to get rid of their rubbish at night by tossing it into his bin. Jo had convinced him to use his degree and he had caved in and enrolled for a teaching qualification. The instruction was lightweight. It didn't seem to matter whether he turned up for tutorials or not, so long as he fulfilled his obligation to teach part-time at the technical school out in the western suburbs. The one good thing about it was meeting the art master, Lang Tzu.

Jo's boss at the antiquarian bookshop had given her three months' maternity leave on full pay. He wasn't required to do this, but he was very fond of Jo and wanted to keep her on. Jo was experiencing the steep mood swings women suffer after the heroic event of childbirth. She cried easily about trivial things and was inclined to lose her temper for trifling reasons. Andy was sitting at the garden table outside the back door of the kitchen, Hennie on his lap, when Jo dropped a mug of tea. The mug shattered, the hot tea going everywhere, the shards scattering across the floor. Jo didn't cry out or curse but stood staring at the pieces of the smashed mug with a look of abject dismay on her face.

Andy said, 'Here, take Hennie, I'll clean it up.'

It was Jo's favourite mug. The one her aunt Hennie had given her for her ninth birthday. A picture of a tabby kitten printed on it. The kitten's disconnected left eye accusing her from the floor. Jo ignored Andy's offer.

When he looked at her he saw that she was weeping. What his mother would have described as sobbing her little heart out. Letting it all come out, as if she'd woken from a dream and found herself alone in a strange place. Lost again.

'It's only a mug, darling,' Andy said.

She stood there in the middle of the kitchen, as alone as anyone can be, in her loose green T-shirt and her short denim skirt, her Greek sandals on her tanned feet, and she wept as if her child had died. Grief-stricken, she was.

Hennie started screaming.

Andy was already feeling a bit shocked at how their lives had turned around so dramatically for them since Hennie's arrival. Jo standing in the middle of the kitchen weeping about her precious broken mug. He had lost his lovely sexy companion. Hennie in his arms squirming and screaming, her face a worrying purple. And she had shat herself, the stench rising to his mouth. He left Jo weeping in the kitchen and carried Hennie upstairs and wiped her clean and put the cream on her bum and changed the nappy. Jo refused to use disposable nappies and Andy found pushing the safety pin in through the thick wad of towelling was dangerous with all the squirming around that was going on. For a six-week-old, Hennie was amazingly strong. She didn't stop screaming and squirming until he'd walked her up and down for a good twenty minutes. When she finally went quiet he saw she was asleep. He lowered her gently into her cot, holding his breath in case he woke her.

He stayed calm. It was something Andy could do. It came naturally to him to remain outwardly calm during a crisis. It was the one gift he was sure of possessing. Inwardly was another matter. They'd had a warning, after all. After their disagreement over the idea of a mortgage they had learned they were no different from anyone else. There had been moments during that period of tension when they had even come close to disliking each other. They didn't talk about it, but they knew they'd lost the pure innocence of their perfect love. Since then they had become more careful with each other. Things were not quite the same as they had been before the house and the baby and his part-time teaching. How could they be?

His ignorance of fatherhood was total. They were feeling their way in the dark, the pair of them, nerves on edge, alert to obstacles and sudden pitfalls. Screams in the night and weeping for no reason, the endless shitty nappies piling up around him demanding the treatment of purification in the bucket of Napisan. After leaving Jo weeping in the kitchen over her broken mug and taking Hennie upstairs to change her nappy, Andy watched Hennie for a while until he was certain she was really asleep. Once she was asleep it was amazing that even sudden loud noises did not usually wake her. She woke when she was hungry: they'd learned that much. Although Jo also knew when Hennie was hungry and sometimes woke her up to ease the pressure of her engorged breasts. It was a wonderfully soothing pleasure for Jo to breastfeed the baby. Watching on, Andy often envied her the almost magical closeness she enjoyed with Hennie, as if their two bodies and their two minds hadn't fully separated at birth but had remained connected, their hearts beating in time as they had done since the beginning. Andy loved them both helplessly, but he knew he stood outside the mysterious intimacy of mother and child. That much was obvious. Seeing the pair of them in perfect harmony, he often felt that he really was on his own. It was even clearer to him now that he would have to find his meaning in the privacy of his writing. It was an admission that daunted him. He had tried and failed and given up what had become a pointless struggle. He no longer wrote but had not abandoned his dream. He just wasn't working at it. He was too busy clearing the backyard and tearing down the damp wallpaper in their bedroom and doing a thousand other things. He was puzzled and conflicted about the whole thing. When was he going to move forward? Was he ever going to move forward? Or was this it? The house and garden and the half-time teaching taking all his attention and energy. There had been none of Aunt Hennie's money left over after the purchase of the house, and they were living week to week. He was further away from being a writer than he had ever been. He lay awake at night wondering how his life had become so complicated. He was no longer in control. Maybe they should have borrowed the money and bought that other house after all. But then Jo would not have felt welcomed by her aunt Hennie's rose.

When he went back downstairs after putting Hennie down, Jo was sitting at the outside table in the sun drinking tea, a plate of toast and marmalade on the table. She had cleared away the broken pieces of the mug. She looked up and smiled as he came through the back door. 'I made some toast. Your tea's here.'

He sat down across from her and took a sip of the tepid tea. 'She went down okay in the end,' he said.

Jo's gentle smile was beatific.

Andy said, 'So you're okay?'

She nodded without looking at him then gave him a glance to indicate that she was struggling but didn't want to talk about it. She sipped her tea and considered the sad little silver birch tree he had planted in a mound he had built up in the middle of the tiny patch of grass. It was no more than half a metre tall and was without leaves, tight little buds along its fragile main stem. More hope than tree.

She said, 'I think we should move to the country.' She was thoughtful awhile, the muted roaring of the traffic out the front along the over-dimensional route that acted as a frontier to the rat flats. But no birdsong.

Andy wanted to make everything in their life a source of happiness for her. It wasn't that she was the most classically beautiful woman he'd ever met, but there was something he would never be able to describe adequately or even understand about her. This deeper sense of what Jo was to him contradicted his other feeling of being alone and separate from her and Hennie. Jo possessed a deep inner quality that was for him a place where he knew, at times like this, that his spirit might be nurtured, a place beside her in which to grow into his real self, the secret, difficult self he knew was inside and which needed to be released so he might become the writer he dreamed of becoming. It wasn't something straightforward and matter-of-fact, but was something he knew in his heart. He knew that

Jo possessed the ability to make sense of his life for him and that he and Hennie had the power to make sense of her life. Alone, after all, he had not been able to find his way. That was the truth. If his father had still been alive, he might have confessed the failure to him in a letter:

> Dear Dad,
> I have stayed true to our old vision but have not found my way yet. With Jo, well, I can tell you, I believe I will at last find my way. I have produced no work to support this faith as yet, but the faith is in me, and as I sit here looking at this woman who two years ago I had not even met, I know she is my true home. I think you had something like this with Mum. You two never had a row. I never heard an angry word between you, not even after the war when you were beaten and wounded in your soul and your sad body and sometimes drank more than was good for us all. Not even then, dear Father, did I ever hear you speak to our mother harshly or in anger, though I often saw you look at her from some great distance, and at those times there was a tear in your eyes that you could not wipe away or disguise. And I was moved to see you like that and knew myself helpless to come between you and your pain. I think you had with our mother what I have found with Jo. She stills the panic in me.

There was that old regret in Andy that as a boy he had failed to find the means to comfort his father in his distress after his return from the front. He had seen then that his father was lost and was unable to revive his faith in art, which might have been a way of escape from the misery that enveloped him and drove him to drink till he was so distant and alone they could no longer reach him. Their loving dad was no more but was a dangerous outsider. It was not Dad who had come home to them, but a bleak-souled stranger from hell. The gentle Dad of old lay dead with his comrades in some faraway field in Europe. But even that was too fanciful. That his father became a whole man again, eventually, Andy was certain was due to the redemptive power of art. Sure, there was the more obvious reason, the reason everyone understood, in the birth of another son, Andy's young brother, Harry. They had no telephone in those days and the birth came on early and passed off without complications. When Andy's father came out of the bedroom in his shirtsleeves with his braces hanging and said to Andy and his sisters, 'Come in and kiss your wee brother,' he was glowing with a kingly rapture that never quite left him afterwards. Was it only due to the arrival of their little brother as his beacon of hope that their father began to paint again? They all thought so, but Andy believed he knew better. Though his father never again suggested he and Andy take a trip out to the enchanted ponds where he had spun the yarn of the old pike. That brief time was gone and would never return, but Andy was glad to have had it with him and to see him now content once again within himself, loving his new son with an ardour and a belief that consoled the family. Andy was glad his father had a few years of that wholeness with the innocence of his art again before he died. He held that knowledge inside himself and was able to remain a believer.

Five years after his brother was born, Andy turned sixteen and knew it was time for him to leave the family and make his own way. The art of his father, that reaching after something unreachable he had spoken of, was the legacy Andy took with him. Wherever he went he made drawings and was often complimented on them and told he should become an artist. But he knew he was not an artist. 'I'll do it in the next life,' he joked. 'I'm not ready for art yet.' For Andy, art stood way out there in a realm of being that inspired him and puzzled him and tempted him. But it did not engulf him. Writing would eventually engulf him, and when it did it was the tragic life of the failed artist Lang Tzu that inspired him.

7

When Hennie was four months old, Jo and Andy were out in the kitchen doing the washing-up one Friday evening after dinner, Jo washing and Andy drying and putting away. Jo stopped suddenly, a saucepan in her hands, and said, 'I'm going to go mad if I have to spend another day alone in the house with her.'

Andy wasn't surprised by this. There had been signs, even though Jo hadn't said anything until now that might have made him think she was anything but happy at home with Hennie. Of course her three months on full pay had come to an end, but they were managing.

'I stand at the window in your workroom up the front and I watch the trucks going by. That's me between feeds and nappy changes, envying those drivers sitting up there smugly in their cabins going somewhere.'

Jo spoke to the nurse at the clinic, who assured her that three mornings a week wasn't going to deprive Hennie of anything essential. 'Your little Hennie will love it at the creche. They all love it.'

So Jo went back to work at Armand Denier's grand premises in King Street, Monday to Wednesday mornings, sitting behind her oak desk in the calm of the book-lined showroom making up Armand's quarterly catalogue, *Australia, America & the Pacific*, on her IBM golf ball typewriter and forgetting for considerable moments of time that she was even a mother, lost in the romantic detail of the old volumes: *A Voyage round the World in His Britannic Majesty's Sloop, Resolution, commanded by Capt. James Cook* etc. The priceless volumes open beside her on a bookrack, for her reference, bound in handsome contemporary tree calf. She became lost in the dream of it, then hearing in her mind the sudden sharp cry of her baby was jerked back to the reality of her life. And Diana Tring, tall and thin and nearing her retirement, the austere publishing director of Armand's reprints of Australian documents and early items long out of print, under the imprint Editions Chanticleer, Diana bringing Jo a coffee and finding her wiping her eyes and sniffling, a hanky held to her nose. 'You're crying, darling!' A woman whose love for Jo was a gift to them both. It was Diana Tring's hope that Jo would stick to the job and be appointed the senior editor of her own empire of Editions Chanticleer and eventually take over the reprint side of Armand's business altogether one day. Her own solitary life was infinitely brightened by Jo's presence. She believed in Jo. And Jo loved this other world of her work and had her own secret hopes for it.

And Monday to Wednesday, while Jo was in her delicious other world in the middle of the city, Andy took Hennie to the creche after Jo left to catch the tram in the morning and picked her up again at lunchtime before Jo was due home. Before he went down to the creche to get her at midday, a five-minute walk, he heated the bottle of milk Jo had expressed before leaving. He ran hot water into a saucepan then took the bottle of milk out of the fridge and left it in the saucepan while he walked down Bay Street to the creche to fetch his daughter.

He gave Hennie the bottle in the kitchen. She lay in his arms sucking like a machine, her eyes closed, her little fingers tightly around the bottle. Did she think it was her mother? He looked down at her and smiled, seeing a small eager animal, the nourishment of the mother's milk, the whole grand legend of it in poetry and life. 'You are my daughter,' he whispered to her. And he wondered how it could be that his life had changed so radically. He had not planned this. His own wellbeing now was dependent on this little person's wellbeing. He lived with the steady underlying heart dread that she would not make it through the hazards of existence and achieve a good life. He even wished contentment for her in her old age, that same contentment his mother knew. He would not be there to see it. It was a difficult subject for him. One day he would have to part from his daughter for the last time. The thought was unbearable. Had his own mother known the same dread in her heart? Had he been the cause of that dread? He bent down and sniffed Hennie's scalp, his eyes closed, the sound of her mad sucking loud in his ear.

In the couple of fleeting hours before lunchtime he worked at things like replacing broken and cracked glass panes in various windows and fixing the front gate. Always a dozen other jobs crying out for his attention. The big ones of improving the bathroom and the kitchen. Then there was each day's crop of stinking nappies to be dealt with in the washhouse under the fragrant Félicité et Perpétue. There never quite seemed to be the uninterrupted slab of hours they had planned for, when his mind was to be clear of the next thing, so that he could settle deep into his own other world. He didn't have his own world. Nowadays he found himself looking forward to lunch at the pub with Lang on Thursdays as the highlight of his week. His secret hope for that great friendship. He didn't confess this to Jo but insisted, when she asked, that he was loving being at home, and especially when he was alone with Hennie. Jo wasn't convinced. But she let it go. And anyway, it was often the truth.

Timing was everything for Jo and Andy these days. Their carefully worked-out schedule was critical. They couldn't afford to miss a beat. They became a finely tuned team. Or they didn't. The routine didn't always work perfectly. Jo was supposed to get home on Wednesday in time for Andy to hand over Hennie and catch the tram to the school in Brunswick. Technically this was possible. In practice it turned out to be difficult to achieve and it was often touch and go. He was frequently late for his first afternoon class. Life could become a bit breathless at those times. He had once prided himself on the claim that he was never in a hurry. When he and Lang were late back from the pub, the vice-principal covered for Lang and didn't make a fuss—it seemed that the two of them were old pals and had an understanding—but Andy knew the full-time young teachers resented him and his easygoing attitude to his classes. Some of them had young children of their own but they were almost never late for class. They all worked full-time and took their careers seriously.

At the bar on Thursday, Lang suggested Andy might like to go with him to an art auction. 'You might find it interesting.' Andy said he'd like that, but Lang didn't make a specific date for this.

Lang asked Andy where his interest in art came from. Andy told him about his father and their painting excursions into the country and how art had come to mean something precious to him as a boy. 'Dad had an untroubled attitude to his painting and drawing. It was a simple pleasure for us both. A chance for us to be together, just the two of us. Dad never saw art as a challenge. There was no struggle in it. We never really talked about what it meant to us. We just did it. Together. It was something deeply innocent and believed in by both of us. I've never been able to separate my feelings about art from my love for my father. Whenever I think of art or see a painting I like, I see an image of my dad painting and sketching out in the country, standing in the shade under an old oak tree lost in his observation of the landscape around him, or watching the ripples on the water of a pond. He never did pictures of people. It was always landscapes. I look at art through my father's eyes.'

Lang said, 'You're lucky to have had a friendship like that with your father. It was my mother and my grandfather who taught me the traditional arts of calligraphy and painting. I scarcely knew my father. My father couldn't have cared less about art.' He looked at his watch. 'Have we got time for another?'

'Sure, why not?'

'How about coming out to my place for a drink tonight?' Lang said. 'You can have a look at my collection. I'd like to hear what you think.'

Lang ordered another round and asked Dom for a piece of paper and a pen. The barman was sitting at the end of the bar marking up his horses for the Tote as usual. Without speaking he tore a page from his notebook and passed it down the bar to Lang along with his pen, keeping his eyes on the form guide on the bar in front of him. Lang wrote his address and telephone number on the piece of paper and handed it to Andy. 'Come out after you and Jo have had your dinner.' He passed the biro back to Dom. 'If you can't make it, that's fine. Just let me know.'

That evening, after Jo had fed Hennie and got her off to sleep, she dished up Andy's favourite leek-and-potato soup. He thanked her and said, 'I can't help wondering if Lang gave up painting because of the racism.' It was Lang's slightly defensive tone when he said, *If you can't make it, that's fine*, that made Andy wonder about this.

Jo said, 'So ask him. He's your friend, isn't he?'

But it wasn't that simple for Andy and it was also obvious from her abrupt tone that Jo was tired and in no mood for talking about Lang and his problems, so he said no more and they ate their soup in silence. Sometimes he and Jo couldn't talk to each other openly about their feelings. This was one of those times, and Andy was wondering if she was resenting the idea of him abandoning her for the evening. Their evenings together had been kind of sacred.

He cleared his throat. 'Do you mind me going out to see Lang tonight?'

'Why would I mind?' She didn't look at him. 'We're grown-ups, aren't we?'

'It's just that if I don't take Lang up on this invitation, I'm afraid he may not invite me to his home again. I'm not sure of where the boundaries are with him. If I make an excuse not to visit, he might think I'm being racist.'

'What nonsense!'

'Consider it: since the age of ten, Lang has been living in a country where he was officially described in the White Australia policy as a member of an unwelcome and despised race. It's only a couple of years ago that Whitlam finally did away with it. It's not nothing.'

'Just go and see him, for God's sake,' Jo said irritably. 'Why are you making such a stupid fuss about it?'

As they did the washing-up, Jo was still closed off and silent. The way she set the dishes down after drying them, as if they had wronged her and she would have loved nothing more than to have thrown them violently at the wall. Andy hated the weight of her silence.

THE DEAL

When he was leaving, he said, 'I won't be late.'

She kissed him coldly and said, 'It's okay. You should go. I want you to go.' It was a lie. They hadn't been apart a single evening since Hennie's birth. 'Invite him over for a meal.' She laughed at her own bravado. 'It's good that one of us has a friend.'

8

Driving to the address in Camberwell that Lang had given him, Andy was feeling guilty for leaving Jo alone with Hennie. But it was that last remark of hers as he left that had him thinking to himself, *Jo has a child, her own house, a job she loves, and she's got me. Is it so bad if I have a friend?* It did change things, he had to admit that. They had met as loners, his family unseen for years in England, the last of her family dying or whereabouts unknown. They had each found their life partner with the other, and had then become a family with a house. All that was true.

Now he was wondering, really for the first time, how well he and Jo knew each other. They loved each other, there was no doubt about that, but did they *know* each other? Going out to drink with Lang in the evening was behaving in the old, free way. Jo couldn't even pretend to do that. Jo was stuck with Hennie's feeding pattern, whether she liked it or not. He remembered now, not long after they'd moved in and she was going through a low period, she had a cry and when he pressed her to tell him what the matter was she said angrily, 'I'm trapped!' He didn't know how to respond. *He* wasn't trapped. He understood then that he and Jo weren't really equals anymore. It hadn't occurred to him till then. Going out on his own in the evening and leaving her alone with the baby wasn't fair. He knew this. But he didn't turn around and go back. He told himself it was just for an hour or two. He even said aloud, 'It's no big deal. What's the fuss about?' Secretly, however, he knew he was enjoying a freedom Jo no longer had.

He found the address and parked under a streetlight. He stepped out and stood by the car, getting his bearings. There was no traffic. There were no other cars parked in the street. A sense of privacy and affluence. A dog barked somewhere. It had been raining again, fine and calm now after a storm earlier in the evening. The mature London planes lining both sides of the street.

Number twenty-seven was a single-storey house of dark red brick from the Edwardian era. It was set well back from the street behind a low brick wall that came up to the level of Andy's knees. Unlike the smartly manicured gardens of the neighbouring houses, Lang's garden was an unkempt patch of grass and weeds. A wrought-iron front gate was chained and padlocked, as if the owner had left and did not intend returning anytime soon. Beyond the gate, lanky cotoneasters hung halfway across the drive, all but obscuring from Andy's view the doors of the garage at the far end, leaves and twigs on the old brickwork of the driveway. The garage was a separate construction beside the left-hand wall of the house. Its wooden doors seemed once to have been painted green, the paint now faded and flaked, the weight of the doors causing them to sag towards the centre. They did not appear to have been opened for years. Though never as grand as either of its neighbours, Lang's house must nevertheless once have been the proud residence of a respectable middle-class family. The central porch was flanked by generous bay windows on both sides. The glow of a low light in one of the front rooms and another yellowish lamp in the porch. In each of the bay windows there were several coloured glass panels. In the softly lit window on the left Andy made out pictures of Australian native animals. Kangaroos and a kookaburra and maybe a koala and the sharp outlines of the black-and-white plumage of magpies. A large terracotta dragon adorned the crest of the pitched slate roof above the porch. The exotic beast was crouched in silhouette against the evening sky. At first Andy thought it must be a Chinese dragon, but on second thought decided it was more likely a European dragon of the kind slain by Saint George. It sat there on its haunches, brooding and ill-tempered, its wing bones poking up sharply. Beware of the dragon!

He stepped over the low wall into the garden at the place where an area of rank grass and weeds had been trodden down, though a large dock weed had resisted, still standing proudly above the slaughter. Did delivery men also clamber over the wall? He walked across to the porch. Before he'd had a chance to ring the bell, he saw a shadow approaching through an oval window set in the door at head height. The glass in the oval window was textured with little wavelets, so that the shadowy movement of the figure seemed to rise and fall as it came towards the door. Andy didn't ring the bell but waited. He heard Lang cough.

Lang opened the door. 'Thank you for coming, Andy. I've been waiting for you.' He spoke as if he had rehearsed his greeting. 'I thought you might decide not to come after all. It's a long way for you to drive and you have your baby to care for.' He stepped back and invited Andy inside. Before closing the door he hesitated, as if he were not sure of his next move, then he gave in to the impulse and looked out into the garden, checking first to the left side then the right. Only after performing this ritual inspection twice did he close the door and join Andy in the hall.

Andy said playfully, 'Did you think there might be a robber lurking out there?'

'I've been robbed twice.' Lang looked at him and smiled. It was a smile that seemed to affect only one side of his features, the other side, the left side, withholding judgement, on Andy and on the friendship. It was his eyes and his lips that determined this effect. His left eye drooped a fraction, just enough to cause Andy's gaze to linger on it for a moment, as if he asked a question of Lang. How sincere really was his welcoming smile, or was he holding an uncertainty in reserve? Lang's lips, which were full and even sensuous, likewise expressed something of this ambivalence, the right side of his lips lifting with the welcoming smile, while the left side, like his left eye, hesitated to join in.

They didn't shake hands or embrace.

The air was heavy with the smell of cigarettes and alcohol. It was an unventilated staleness, a smell that must have taken years to become ingrained in the fabric of the house. Rooms off the hallway gave an impression of being undisturbed. It was the home of a lonely man. Lang's manner lacked the confidence of their meetings in the pub. Andy did not feel at ease.

He avoided Lang's scrutiny and looked to his left through the bevelled glass panels of a pair of double doors that led off the hall into a sitting room. The room beyond the doors was richly furnished in the English style, lit by a bronze lamp standing on a darkly polished side table in the deep bay of the window. Beside the lamp a tall glass vase filled with a desiccated arrangement of hydrangea blooms from which the original colour had been lost and replaced by the uniform grey of something long dead. Andy thought of the kind of thing seen in cemeteries, the bereaved forgetting to freshen their memorial to the dead, or maybe dead themselves. A fine head-and-shoulders portrait of a beautiful dark-haired woman gazed directly back at him from the wall above the fireplace. The woman was half turned away, looking back over her shoulder, as if she were on the point of leaving, her gaze filled with regret, longing and uncertainty.

The door across the hall from the lit sitting room was closed. Lang led him across the hall and along a broad passage. The walls of the passage were hung with framed paintings and drawings; another door on the right-hand side was closed. For a second Andy thought two people were coming towards them, then he realised it was their own reflections in a large Victorian gilt-framed mirror above a low table at the end of the passage. There was a single pale yellow vase on the table.

At the mirror, the passage made a sharp left-hand turn, after which it narrowed. Here the walls were bare of pictures. This section of passage was no more than ten metres long, the ceiling lower, a closed door ahead of them. Lang opened the door and Andy followed him into the kitchen. It was a small room, cluttered and stuffy and very warm, a low ceiling with one small window above the sink, its four squares of glass looking out into a back garden, where the naked branches of a tree were caught in the light. The warmth came from a two-bar electric heater standing close beside a deal table. The table was covered with piles of journals and art auction catalogues, dirty plates with half-eaten meals and unwashed glasses and teacups scattered among them. Two glass tumblers, one half filled with red wine, and a cardboard cask of Penfolds claret, a heavy cut-glass ashtray crammed with cigarette butts.

Lang drank the wine in the half-full tumbler with an abrupt movement that made him seem to be alone, then he filled both tumblers with the wine and handed one to Andy.

They touched their glasses, their eyes meeting briefly as they each took a drink. The wine was sharp and faintly warm.

'I want you to give me your opinion of a special painting,' Lang said. 'It's in the sitting room.'

Andy had begun to get the impression that Lang was deeply drunk. He appeared to be playing a role, making an effort to seem sober by being formal.

Lang lit a cigarette from the stub of the one he was smoking and he picked up his tumbler and the cask of wine. 'Bring your glass.'

Andy followed him back along the passage. They went through the glass doors and into the sitting room. The bronze lamp sending its sad little signal out into the great dark night of Camberwell's silence. Furnished with the grace and charm of an old-fashioned world that was long gone, the air in this room was unheated. The undisturbed stillness of a room that was rarely occupied. It was an old world of fine English furniture, comfortably upholstered chairs, Cuban mahogany side tables and elaborate gilt mirrors, and here and there on the walls Australian landscape paintings that Andy's father would have admired. There was no sign of anything Chinese, except for a tall square wooden box on the mantelpiece, several crudely executed Chinese characters on it.

Lang set the wine cask on a low coffee table and turned to face the fireplace. 'There she is.' He pointed at the portrait of the beautiful woman.

Andy wondered if it was by the great English modernist Augustus John. The woman in three-quarter profile and looking back over her shoulder at the viewer. In a more romantic age it might have been titled *The Departure*. Something of the sadness of the final moments of a friendship, or a love affair, the regret or melancholy in her dark eyes. He stood beside Lang admiring the picture.

Lang smoked his cigarette, his eyes narrowed. 'What do you think of her?'

'She's wonderful,' Andy said. 'It's not John, is it?'

Lang laughed. 'It's mine. I painted her. It's the only picture of mine I've kept.' He turned to Andy. 'I burned everything else.'

He was relaxing, permitting the faint euphoria of the drink to show through. 'I painted her and drew her likeness a hundred times that year. This is the last one.' He considered Andy. 'So, you think it's wonderful?'

'Absolutely! Yes, it's superb. I'm hugely impressed. Is it really your work?'

Lang gave a short, ironic laugh, laughing at himself, dismissing the impression that he might believe in his own seriousness, his greatness as an artist, rebuking Andy's disbelief. He gulped down his wine and closed his eyes and breathed a heavy sigh. He had spilled a few drops of the red wine on his pale slacks. He looked shabby, a strangely beautiful lost man, Andy thought, standing there contemplating his past triumph, as if he had dreamed it all long ago. At that moment, Andy felt the lure of Lang's secret life and knew that one day he would find in it his own story. It was a weird, powerful, intoxicating feeling. Then it began to drift away as he thought about it. He would never retrieve the purity of that moment. He said, 'My father would have fallen in love with her.'

'We were all in love with her.' Lang flourished his cigarette. 'Her name was Agatha Hervieu. Agatha!' Lang jabbed his finger at the picture, his hand so close to the canvas Andy feared he might touch the surface of the paint with the lit cigarette he was clutching between his fingers. 'We met at the Gallery School. After we graduated, I got so drunk I asked her to marry me. It was in the early hours of the morning. The trams had started and it was getting light. She was sitting on a bench in the Treasury Gardens. A crowd of us had gone there to drink after the pubs closed. She didn't look up to see who was proposing marriage to her. I could have been any of us, man or woman. She murmured indifferently, *Okay.*'

He fell silent, moved by his recollection of the night and Agatha, the days of his youth.

'Yes, we were all in love with her. We were in awe of her distinction. She was the best of us.' He drank and smoked and squinted at his painting, as if he might yet decide to burn it. 'She didn't get any of the awards. That painting was shortlisted for the Crouch Prize. The Crouch was the most important art prize in Australia in those days. The shortlisting kept my hopes alive for years.' He turned around and refilled his glass at the low table and lit another cigarette, desperate, sad, remembering, drunk. 'The Crouch shortlisting was the height of my fame.' He laughed, a sour, bitter laugh, and emptied the wine down his throat.

Andy listened to Lang's voice going on, elaborating memory, and he looked at the painting of the hauntingly beautiful Agatha, the woman on the point of leaving.

Lang suddenly fell silent.

There was a low buzzing sound from somewhere.

Andy said, 'So how do you get on with your neighbours here?'

'Some years ago, one of them called the police. Two policemen came to my door that Saturday afternoon. The older policeman asked me politely if I was all right. I said, *Yes, I'm happy, thank you for asking me.* He was nice. He smiled at his mate and said to me, *If you ever have any trouble, call the station and I'll see to it for you.* I asked him why they had called on me. He said it had been noticed by one of my neighbours that my gate was always closed and chained shut and my grass was never mowed.'

Andy said, 'The bastards couldn't just come in and ask you how you were going. They called the fucking cops! Jesus!'

'The older of the two policemen was gracious.'

Andy said, 'Camberwell! How can you bear to live out here?'

Lang gave a sly little smile and pointed his finger up at the ceiling. 'I've got a dragon on my roof.' He bent down and turned on the gas at the wall then struck a match and held it to the gas. There was a satisfying pop and the blue flame ran quickly across the width of the fire. The warmth was immediate. They both watched the fire, the bars behind the flames beginning to glow a convincing orange. 'It gets cold in here,' Lang said.

The chill of disuse and absence. The heavy antique English furniture, the mirrors reflecting imaginary depths and shadowed corners, it all had the look of having been undisturbed for years. And nothing Chinese, except that tall box on the mantelpiece. Andy felt as if they were intruders. Their voices flattened by the embedded silence. There was no accumulation of dust.

Andy said, 'It really is a lovely portrait, Lang. It wouldn't be out of place in the National Gallery.'

Lang said nothing.

'Did you really destroy all your other work?'

Lang said again, kind of sheepishly, 'So, you think she's beautiful?'

'Oh yes, she's magnificent. But so sad. I imagine she's about to go to the station and catch a train that's going to carry her away from her loved ones and her home for the last time. She is willing herself to turn and look back squarely at everyone and everything that is familiar to her and which she is leaving behind forever. It is all there in her gaze. There is this sad and beautiful story in her gaze. It's a great achievement, Lang.'

Lang laughed. 'You know something about art but you're a romantic.' He was silent, smoking and looking at the portrait, dragging on his cigarette. 'She didn't love me.' He gave a little inward chuckle, a small expression of self-mockery, a kind of signature for him whenever he was talking about something intimate to himself, something personal and touched by deeply felt emotions from his past. His reality seemed to be entirely in the past, a golden, beautiful, longed-for, past that he would never recapture but would strive to find within himself, a striving after something unattainable, an old habit of mind that would never be outgrown, the habit of mind of the artist. And the suffering then, a suffering with hope at its heart in those days.

Andy saw in him the subject of his own longings. His own ordinary life a kind of grey expanse of nothing but what everyone else expected: a wife, a house, a child. Lang would never settle for that. Never.

'We became husband and wife,' Lang said. 'A married couple. We worked. We painted. We made our art and we drank. In those days we all drank at the Swanston Family Hotel. The misfits were at home there. It was where the homeless among us found a home. The Swanston belonged to us. The seers and prophets, the poets, the artists, the halfwits and the mad magicians, we all drank there. There were fights. Loud, fierce disagreements. Of course there were! And punch-ups. We laughed at them. But they were within the family. We were safe with one another. It was our community. It is all gone now. All that. The beautiful wine bars too. Bolte and his minister of morality, Mr Rylah, closed them down or demolished them. They were jealous of our freedom. They couldn't stand to see us happy. It was another age. Agatha was one of us, but she remained aloof. She was contemptuous of the crowd.' He chuckled again, the memory alive in him, gnawing at him.

He was half a head shorter than Andy. Andy had an image of him standing beside the glorious woman of the portrait, his beautiful wife Agatha, she taller than he, the two of them an unlikely couple. Were they lovers? Andy could not imagine it. He didn't want to imagine it.

'Agatha and I found a haven with each other. I don't have anything of hers to show you. She threw out all her work and gave up painting long before I did. I believe she was overcome by the futility of the struggle.' He fell silent, smoking his cigarette and contemplating Agatha's parting gaze. 'She was gifted. She gave it all up. *What's the point?* she said, and she shrugged and turned away from it. She was amazing. That was all the explanation I ever got from her: *What's the point?* She was the best of our year. She didn't win any of the awards. She lived in a cloud of unknowing. Her achievement was her solitude. It eclipsed her art. She was great. She was tragic. I loved her. I still love her. We knew ourselves inferior. Our admiration was tainted with the dismay she aroused in us. The truth shone in her.'

He raised the tumbler to his lips and as he drank he grimaced. Although there were deep and comfortable armchairs on both sides of the coffee table, Lang lowered himself carefully to the floor, first squatting then managing to sit, cross-legged and leaning towards the fire, clutching his tumbler of wine in his left hand and a cigarette in his right.

Andy sat on the floor beside him and listened to his monologue of memories.

'Sickert, not John,' Lang said. 'Sickert was the greatest of them. I'll show you. A nude painted against the light, her back to the viewer, gazing at the thinly curtained window in front of her. We don't know who she is. She is no one. Her identity is erased. She is simplified to suit the artist's lust. She is Sickert's fantasy. An artist's fantasy. It is grotesque. But it is true. Sickert had the terrible courage of the truth in his brush. She is the secret dream of every man. I would be satisfied if I could own such a painting. That would be it for me. The end of collecting. The end of art. The end of the helpless longing. You don't know what it means to me!'

He waved his hand, dismissing his obsession, a slop of wine spilling onto the rug.

'Agatha would never have people in the house. If I ever had a friend over she kept out of the way until he had gone. When the weather was fine she sat in the back garden under the pear tree and smoked. Agatha sitting in the garden on a mild evening, the smoke of her cigarette in the air, gazing off into her thoughts. She always had a book with her. A novel. George Sand or Duras. In French. Agatha's father was French. She was brought up speaking two languages. If I asked her what she was reading, she handed me the book and got up and walked off and did something else, or did nothing, and returned later and picked up her book again. I can see her sitting out there whenever I look out of the kitchen window.' He turned to Andy. 'I didn't know why she agreed to marry me or why she stayed with me as long as she did. Indifference, I suppose. Her motives were concealed. I envied her this impressive detachment. French novels were her salvation. Do you read French? I don't.'

He said with feeling, 'I am waiting for her to come home. She will come back to me when she is old. This is the only home Agatha ever found. The only place where her silence and her solitariness were not challenged. With me, she never had to explain herself. She will remember this place when she is a frail old woman and will return and reclaim her place in it. She knows she will not have to account for herself to me.

I shan't ask her a single question about where she has been or what she has accomplished during the years of her absence.'

He talked about Agatha for a long time. Most of it was rambling conjecture about what might have been. Andy eventually looked at his watch. The fire and the wine were making him sleepy. 'I'm sorry, Lang—I'll have to go. Jo will be worrying. I promised her I wouldn't be late. She'll be wondering where I've got to. She's been a bit edgy since Henrietta came along.' He immediately regretted saying this. It felt like a betrayal of Jo.

Lang came out of his trance and put his hand on Andy's arm, then took it away again at once, as if he had forgotten himself. 'We'll just have one last drink.'

'I can't, honestly.'

'A toast.'

'To what?'

'To Agatha.'

He refilled Andy's empty tumbler. They clinked their glasses and Lang looked steadily into Andy's eyes and said, 'Agatha.'

Andy murmured, 'Agatha.' He was wondering if Lang was taking this solemn toast as some kind of a pledge. A vow even. Lang had injected a seriousness into his voice that drew on a deeper level of commitment than Andy had expected from him. Perhaps it was partly due to the effect of the wine, but there was something almost hypnotic in Lang's company.

Andy found this attractive but also a little frightening, as if he might find himself being drawn into a relationship that would lead to places he might not want to go. Places Jo would find foreign. He thought of the cliché *Be careful what you wish for.* Andy was wary suddenly, and aware of his own ambivalence in both wanting a deeper and grander friendship with Lang and fearing it at the same time. The thought in his head at that moment was, *What might I be letting myself in for?*

Lang saw Andy to the door and stood and watched until Andy was in his car, then he still stood, waiting until the car had driven away and the street had returned to its silence. When the sound of Andy's car had been swallowed by the night, Lang took a look around, then closed the door and went back into the front room and turned off the gas fire. He picked up his tumbler and the wine cask and stood looking at Agatha looking back at him from her moment of departure. Then he switched off the light and returned to the kitchen. He stood at the window over the sink looking out into the night, the bare branches of the pear tree. Nothing moved. He turned away from the window and sat at the table and lit a cigarette, then refilled his glass and drank the wine. Maria would come in the morning and let herself in and he would remain in bed until he heard her leave again. She would move silently from room to room, like a shadow, with her dusters. She knew how to behave in Lang's house. He leafed through an old Sotheby's catalogue from London.

It was getting light by the time Lang went to bed. He left the money for Maria on the table in the hall, weighting it with a little bronze lion, then he went into his bedroom and closed the door. Hanging on the wall behind his bedhead was a large, intricate pencil drawing of a tree fern gully in the Dandenongs by the early colonial artist Eugene von Guérard. The drawing was highly detailed. A botanical study. A professional botanist would not have faulted it. Lang sat on his bed smoking a final cigarette and looking towards a tall chest of drawers against the far wall. Resting on top of the chest of drawers, its covers pale against the dark wood, was George Sand's novel *La ville noire*, the blue edge of a bookmark just visible. He hadn't found a way of introducing his idea to Andy after all. He would talk to him about it at the pub. It was easier at the pub.

He bent down and untied the laces on his shoes and took his shoes off and put them side by side under the bed. Then he took off his pants and hung them on the back of the chair that stood beside the bed. His legs were thin and pale, the skin shiny and hairless, like the legs of a young boy. He finished undressing and got into bed and reached and turned off the light. He lay awake watching the light coming up around the edges of the curtains, rehearsing in his mind how he would introduce the topic of his plan to Andy. Every now and then he murmured something aloud, as if he had forgotten he was alone. Then, at last, he went to sleep. We shall never know what he dreamed that night.

9

Jo led the way up the street. She was pulling their new shopping trolley. The footpath was too narrow for them to walk side by side. Andy was bringing up the rear with the pram. On Saturday mornings they went to the South Melbourne Market. The plan was to do the shopping for the entire week. Which meant working out a menu for seven dinners. Lunch was easy, but the evening meal was always a question. Andy had several dishes he liked to cook: lemon chicken with Greek chips, spanakopita, and three kinds of soup. Jo was more inventive, and in addition to numerous meat-based dishes she had a wide repertoire of salads. Andy would never have thought of making a mixed salad with the feature being cheese fried in oil until it was a lovely golden brown and looked more like pastry. Salty and very tasty. Halloumi. Presumably also Greek in origin, like their neighbours.

Jo pulled up at the cafe on the corner across from the market. She parked the trolley beside a vacant table on the wide corner footpath. The trolley was red-and-green tartan. Andy had wanted black or grey, but they'd run out of those non-colours. He sat at the table and looked into the pusher. Hennie was still deeply asleep, swaddled in her pink-and-blue blanket, her little face puckered into a puzzled frown. Was she dreaming? A greyhound on a leash pushed its long snout into the pram and checked out Hennie with him. The owner apologised and drew the dog away. The market stalls on the other side of the road were busy. All vegetables and fruit, one or two stallholders calling out their specials for the morning, a young Chinese girl walking up and down with a tray of strawberries. The sun was shining, a light breeze from the south, almost a spring day, calm, the air filled with market smells and coffee and the sounds of people and traffic, an unbroken stream of cars coming around the corner and heading for the ramp to the rooftop parking.

Jo came out of the cafe and looked into the pram. She reached in and adjusted Hennie's blanket then pulled out the chair next to Andy and sat down. She looked up at the sky. 'It's going to be perfect for a picnic in the Botanic Gardens.' She turned to Andy. 'Do you want to do that?'

'This is too good to miss. Let's make a sandwich or get something from the deli.'

She poked around in her bag. 'Have you got the list?'

'Didn't you have it?'

A young woman came out of the cafe, set down their lattes and turned to leave.

Jo put a hand on her arm. 'I ordered an escargot?'

The young woman drew breath. 'It's coming.' She went back into the cafe.

Andy said, 'Now she hates you.'

'They bring the coffee and then forget to bring what you're having with it till after you've finished your coffee. Why can't they bring them at the same time? What's so difficult about that? I gave the list to you. I'm sure I did.'

Andy stood up and went through the pockets of his jeans and then the pockets of his jacket. 'Nope. A hanky. That's it.'

'It's not in your wallet?'

He took out his wallet again and checked it more thoroughly. The shopping list was neatly folded in with a few notes. He handed it to Jo. 'Sorry.'

Jo took the list and started going through it, at the same time reaching for her coffee and taking a sip.

THE DEAL

Andy took a drink of the coffee and looked around at the people. In the few minutes since they arrived all the spare tables had filled up. A couple with a two- or three-year-old were pretending not to notice their kid making its way under the table of the people next to them. The kid was pulling at the pants of the man, who was gently batting its hand away and frowning. The father of the kid held the broad pages of *The Age* up in front of his face. He was smiling; the mother of the child was glaring at him.

Jo said, 'So Lang has not only erased his wife's identity, but is obsessed with owning a picture of a naked woman who has no identity.'

Andy looked away from the kid under the table. It had found something to eat. 'That's a bit unfair, isn't it? Agatha was obviously like that.'

'So he says. What would Agatha say? Where's that escargot? You go and ask her. I might say something.'

'Here she comes.'

The young woman plonked down a plate with an escargot on it, turned abruptly and strode back into the cafe. Andy laughed. 'Body language.'

'It's not Agatha's story; it's Lang's. She probably left him because she could see there was no room for her reality in his world.' She tore the escargot into two more or less equal parts and took a large bite out of one of the halves. 'Lang belongs to another age,' she said. She reached for her coffee and drained the last drop. 'He's living in a fantasy world.'

Andy bit into his half of the escargot. Hennie was moving and making disgruntled sounds. Jo going through the shopping list beside him. He looked into his coffee cup. Just a sludge of brown froth on the bottom. He said, 'We've become ordinary.'

Jo didn't look up from the list. 'We've always been ordinary.'

'At least Lang's not ordinary.'

She made a noise through her nose.

'He's had an interesting life.'

'Not interesting enough for Agatha to hang around. We should get some of those strawberries that girl's selling.'

'I'd like to write his life story. You're right. He's from another age. We shouldn't judge the past from our point of view now.'

'Why not?'

'Do you think I could have another coffee? Would you like one?'

'We judge the past by living today according to different standards. Have one. I won't. She's starting to fidget. We'd better make a move.'

'That kid under the table will crawl out into the traffic or get bitten by one of these dogs.'

THE DEAL

Jo stood up and reached into the pram. She lifted Hennie out and held her in her arms and jiggled her gently while gazing at her with love. 'You're so beautiful!' She leaned in and kissed Hennie's gleaming forehead. 'Do you want to grab the nappies and the cream out of the pram?'

'Are you going to change her here?'

'Where else?'

'They don't have a changing room over at the market?'

'They're talking about it.'

He pulled the change bag from the pram and handed it to her. He gave the man at the next table a smile. The man looked away. Jo was unwrapping Hennie on the table.

Andy said, 'There's a bench down the end of the street by the station. I don't think you should change her on the table.'

They gathered their things and Jo headed off with Hennie in the pram, making her way towards the bench that stood against the wire fence at the end of the street. Andy went into the cafe and paid their bill. When he caught up with Jo he said, 'Lang's an important part of our social history. His story is part of who *we* are.'

Jo was holding the ends of the fresh nappy together. 'Can you hand me the safety pin?'

Andy gave her the pin and stood watching her fix the nappy. How did she slip the pin through that wad of thick material so easily?

'Anyway,' he said, 'you haven't met him. Maybe he has erased the women in his life the way our society has erased the Chinese from our culture.'

She lifted Hennie up and held her at arm's length. Hennie was smiling. 'Don't worry, darling, Mummy and Daddy aren't going to erase you.' She leaned down and put Hennie into the pram. 'You've made it sound as if he lives in a museum of a past that never was.' She straightened up. 'Get a couple of punnets of those strawberries. We can try them instead of mashed banana.' She turned the pram around and headed towards the market.

Andy followed with the tartan trolley. He was wondering if Lang and Agatha had ever made love. It seemed unlikely. Lang probably never saw Agatha naked.

The strawberry girl had sold out. She was back at the constant business of keeping the shelves fully stocked with lovely displays of glossy fruit. Her father was a slim, fit-looking man in his forties, his double-sized stall the most successful at the front end of the market. The wife-mother of the enterprise sat behind the cash counter. It was self-service, but they had it organised so that customers entered from the station end and exited towards the main street. A natural flow that very few ever went against. The three daughters were all attractive and busy restocking and arranging. Andy stood admiring them. They were probably going to be lawyers or doctors. He was still thinking about Lang. Jo was right, but it wasn't just the women in Lang's life whose personalities had been erased; Lang's whole life in Australia since the age of ten had been about erasure. His decision on his arrival at the school in Ballarat to get rid of everything Chinese, to forget his past and replace it with an Australian identity. Self-erasure. His failure to become an Australian artist deeply fascinated Andy. He knew he could not simply forget it. He thought Jo's insistence that Lang's obsession with owning a Sickert nude represented Lang's fantasy of Agatha's nakedness could be true: his obsession with something he could never have. Andy couldn't see that there was anything bad about having such a fantasy, whereas Jo seemed to think it invalidated Lang's idea of his reality. For Andy, Lang's Sickert fantasy made him more interesting.

10

Lang stopped coming to the school. When Andy called him he got a message. The voice was a woman's: *You have called Lang Tzu. Please leave your number.* Andy drove over there one afternoon. After ringing the bell and knocking on the door and calling down the letter slot a few times, he gave up and drove home. When he asked the vice-principal if she knew anything, she said, 'Lang has taken some time off.' When he asked her if he was okay, she said she believed so, but wouldn't tell him anything more. He didn't know whether to be worried or not. During the lunch break he went to the pub on his own. Dom pulled a beer for him and went back to his seat at the end of the bar. Andy took a drink and watched Dom studying his form guide. 'You haven't seen Lang, I suppose?'

The barman looked up, a deep frown of fierce concentration twisting his features into an ugly mask. He stared at the far wall for a full half-minute. 'Nope,' he said emphatically and went back to studying the horses. His manner said, *Don't talk to me, I'm busy.*

Andy said, 'Me neither.' He downed the rest of his beer and left the bar.

There was no one about in the street. The noise of the kids in the playground filled the air with a distant roaring, as if a tribe of wild men were approaching. It had been a lot more peaceful in the electrical fittings warehouse.

Two months went by and he heard no more about Lang. He told Jo he might quit teaching. 'I'm really just keeping order there. Most of those kids should be out working. They'd be a lot happier.' Andy and Jo held a party for Hennie. She was waking in the night a lot more, teething. Jo's boss, Armand Denier, and his publishing director, Diana Tring, bought her an oversized teddy bear. Jo bought her a set of teething toys to chew on.

The silver birch tree on the mound he'd created was thriving. They called the mound 'the hill'. Behind the mound, concealing the old outside dunny and the toolshed, he erected a timber screen. He had laid ready-made turf over the hill and over the rest of the patch. Outside the back door he set a square of old bricks he'd scavenged from the rubble. They had a green French folding table and two garden chairs which they found in a second-hand shop in Bay Street and put out on the brick square. When the weather was fine they drank their morning coffee sitting at the table, and watched the grass and detected the first signs of growth in the silver birch. Andy worked on the kitchen ceiling. The old plaster was cracked and falling away. He took it all down and replaced it with timber liner boards, which he painted with a light wood stain. The floor in the sitting room was rotten from rising damp in two of the corners, and the single window that looked out onto the side lane was threatening to fall out whenever they tried to open it. Boys from the flats across the road came over and stole the hose he attached to the tap out the front. When he went out to get into the car they called out insults to him and laughed. He waved back at them. He drove to the hardware store. He felt as if the routine of their ordinary lives had swallowed him whole. He was Jonah in the belly of the whale, being slowly digested by domesticity. Each evening he drank a whole bottle of shiraz by himself. Jo was still breastfeeding Hennie at night and had given up drinking.

Lang's disappearance troubled him deeply. He thought about Lang while he was working on the house. Jo said it was unhealthy and he was becoming morbidly obsessed by his loss of the friendship. Jo was worried about him and said so. She suggested he write some more short stories. 'Just sit down and do it. You know you can.'

He said he was fine. But he asked himself, *Am I really a writer? Writers write. I just think about it. I'll be forty in December and all I've ever published is a couple of short stories in little magazines.* His mind was empty. There was no subject in it for a novel except for the life and times of Lang Tzu. But how could he possibly do that? Lang had disappeared. The idea of making something up did not appeal to Andy.

It was late one warm Friday evening. Andy was in the kitchen doing the washing-up when the phone rang in the hall. Jo had gone to bed earlier. She had been overdoing it. Working late editing the letters of a Scottish girl who'd married a Western District settler, a collection in Armand Denier's possession for decades which Diana Tring had handed over to Jo. It was an exciting new responsibility for her and she was taking it very seriously. Several times she'd been held up at work and hadn't made it home in time for him to get the tram to the school for his first class.

When the phone rang, Andy dried his hands on the tea towel and went out to the hall and picked it up.

Lang's voice was hushed and conspiratorial. 'Can you come over?'

'Jesus, Lang! Where the fuck have you been?'

'I'm sorry, Andy. Don't be angry. I can explain.'

Andy waited.

'Will you come over?' Lang sounded like a lost child, not pleading exactly but contrite.

Andy went to the kitchen and finished the washing-up, then he went upstairs. Jo was sitting up in bed reading *The Letters of Rachel Henning*. She was using the famous book as a guide to how she might arrange the Scottish girl's collection. When Andy came into the bedroom he went over to the other side of the bed and looked into the cot. They had brought it into their room after Hennie began waking in the night with her gums on fire. 'How has she been?'

'She loves her new teddy.'

'It won't smother her, will it? Did it have to be so big? Is that a French thing?'

Jo set the book facedown on her thighs and looked up. 'Was that him?'

'Unbelievable!'

'But you're going over there.'

'You were supposed to be resting.'

'This book is restful. Are you going to see him now?'

'I need to. Do you mind that much?'

'Yes, for your sake I mind a lot. For *our* sake.'

THE DEAL

'I won't be late.'

'It's already late. You don't hear from him for two months, then suddenly you've got to see him in the middle of the night? You don't think he might be being a bit manipulative, do you?'

11

Driving over to Lang's through the warm evening, heavy traffic along High Street, childless couples taking their pleasures in cafes and theatres and in just being out, Andy was sure Jo was right. Lang was using him in some way he had not understood. It was then, after he had made this decision and was approaching the quiet streets of Lang's suburb, that Andy had the idea of keeping a notebook in which he would record his meetings with Lang. It didn't matter if Lang was being manipulative, he thought. *So what? Aren't we all being manipulative? Working our own private agendas? Searching for answers to our problems in the lives of others?*

THE DEAL

When he turned into Lang's street, a large, bright blue American car was pulling away from under the streetlight outside the house. Andy parked in the spot the car had vacated and stepped out. He stood listening. The night was still and silent. The front door of Lang's house was wide open, light streaming out onto the rank grass and weeds in the neglected garden. The dragon's shape on the rooftop outlined in the moonlight. Andy had the strange impression that there was no one in the house. An uncanny conviction that they had driven off in the American car. The feeling that he was too late, like a benign dream beginning to slide towards the sinister. He stepped over the wall and walked across the garden and into the porch, where the air from the open door was rich with the smell of Lang's life. He had missed it, the smell of stale tobacco and grog. It was the smell of art and story when he was a child, the smell of his father's Digger Shag and stale beer in the bar of the Green Man, where his dad took a pint of black and tan before they caught the bus home from Keston Ponds. And their flat, where he lived with his mother and sisters, the air heavy with the smells of his father and mother. His mother's stout warming on the hob, the smell of her Woodbine cigarette while she read a novel or darned a sock. The coal fire settling. The smell of coal smoke and cooking, the smell of old books. The smell of home. The smell of the world of art and story. As he entered Lang's front door he was greeted by those old reassuring childhood smells. The legend of Lang's defeat, reminding him of his father's defeat when he returned from the war, a broken man. There was something deep and familiar and beautiful about it. It belonged to him. He knew the smell of Lang's life in his own soul.

He went in and closed the door behind him, and he stood in the hall in his own small silence, looking through the glass panels of the double doors into the sitting room on the left, the bronze lamp shedding its gentle light in the room, the portrait of Agatha gazing at him, her head turned, her features in quarter profile, beautiful and sad. And he thought again what a great painting it was, to have caught her likeness in that fleeting moment of her regretful departure. There was luck and there was genius in the achievement. His father had said, *A portrait is always a disclosure of the artist's self.* Andy loved this other world of Lang's. It stimulated in him a desire to write, to find the story latent within its confusion of facts and impressions. It was where he wished to be. To be a familiar of the tragedy of failure and regret. To be its familiar, but not to be a part of it. To be the intimate voyeur of its hidden realities. The suffering of it. He wondered why the beauty and mystique of art and story must always carry the seeds of despair. As if beauty could not exist without reminding us of death. The dead, grey, desiccated blooms of the hydrangeas in their vase, waiting for Agatha's return. The flowers of memory. The flowers of long ago. Was it possible to write of such things with honesty and remain safe from the disaster of failure and despair oneself? How close could he get to that world without becoming its victim? Was the writer, like the artist, also doomed to failure in the reaching after something beyond their grasp? Or could the writer remain at a safe distance and be a commentator on the tragic struggles of others? A mere onlooker? Was that what the writer was? A person outside the dangerous seductions of the world of art?

When he shifted his weight, the gleam of an auburn highlight in the heavy coils of Agatha's hair caught Andy's attention. The wonderful melancholy of her departure, and those memorial flowers, the beauty and the sadness of it. The loss of Agatha that haunted Lang and made of his life something beautiful and sad. Andy knew it to be an authentic place for Lang, this place lodged deeply in his world of art, and he was himself both attracted and repelled by it.

He turned away and went on down the passage. In the kitchen, Lang was standing over by the back door. He was smoking a cigarette and looking out the window into the evening garden. Beyond the window the branches of the pear tree with its few leaves still clinging on, where on balmy days Agatha had sat reading her French novels and smoking. Did she smoke aromatic Gitanes while reading her French novels? Agatha in the company of Duras and the smell of French cigarettes. Would she really come back to Lang one day, pick up her novel and take it out into the garden, light a cigarette and re-enter the dreaming world of her youth? Andy loved it all fiercely. He would guard this side of his life with all his power. He could not bear to lose it to the infernal shrieking of the schoolyard and the turmoil of the classrooms, and the life of being a responsible father and husband.

The kitchen was quiet, Lang with his back to Andy. Andy noticed a rifle leaning in the corner beside the sink. He was very surprised to see it there. It was a small-calibre rifle. He recognised it as a single-shot .22 of a kind they had called a pea rifle in the bush. Had it always been there and he just hadn't noticed it before? Its slim form leaning inconspicuously in the shadow between the window and the door.

He said, 'So what's the idea of the gun?'

Lang spun around. 'You gave me a start!'

'I'm sorry. I thought you would have heard me closing the front door.'

'Sergei's just gone. You missed him. I told him to leave it open for you.'

'I saw him driving off.'

'The rifle belongs to him. He lent it to me a while ago. It was there when you first came here.' He looked at Andy. 'You didn't notice it then?'

'No.'

'It's for me to shoot the feral cat that's living out there in my wilderness. She howls at night. Sergei said I should put out my leftovers if I wanted to get a clean shot at her. But I don't usually have any leftovers, so I bought some tins of cat food. I put some out in a saucer each morning. The saucer is there.' He pointed. 'It's clean. Soon after I started feeding her, I noticed that she had begun to lose her fear of me. She still slinks away if I open the door. She is careful, but if I just stand here at the window looking out, she meets my eye and we gaze at each other for long minutes. I believe she is thanking me. She was here a moment ago. I didn't hear you coming in, but she heard you. She has acute hearing and is always alert. She is a survivor. She has beautiful eyes. Sergei said she's had babies out there somewhere while I was away and is feeding them. Without her, the babies will starve to death.'

Andy had the feeling Lang was talking about the spirit of Agatha when he spoke of the beauty of the cat's eyes.

'We are both outcasts, me and the mother cat.' He laughed shortly and stepped across and reached to the table and crushed his cigarette butt in the big glass ashtray that sat there. Among the butts were two stumps of Black Russian Sobranies, the gold glinting in the overhead light. 'There is nowhere she can call home.'

'So you're not going to shoot her?'

'She trusts me.'

They were both silent.

Lang said, 'How is Jo? Is she any better?'

'Jo's fine. She soon got over her depression.'

Lang lit another cigarette and took a long drink of wine then said, in a slightly guarded voice, as if he feared to mention the subject, 'And how's the kitchen coming on?'

'Yes. It's going okay.' Andy laughed. 'I've done the plumbing myself. I couldn't be bothered waiting any longer.'

'And your writing?'

Andy pulled out a chair and sat at the table. He looked up at Lang, who continued to stand with his back to the heater. 'The VP said you needed some time off.'

Lang sat in the other chair. 'It's complicated. Are you having a drink?'

Andy shrugged and looked at the wine cask. 'Just a small one.'

He watched Lang fill a tumbler to the brim from the cask. Lang turned and handed it to Andy, his hand trembling so that a few drops of the wine spilled onto the table between them. Andy thanked him and took a drink from the glass.

They sat at the table, Lang pushing back the slew of papers and catalogues to make room. The two-bar heater glowing red, the small room stuffy, the air thick with cigarette smoke. The fug and the strong smell of men. He had missed it. The longing in him unsatisfied. He loved Jo and he loved little Hennie and would die for either of them, and when he was not with them he missed them and feared for them. But at times he feared to be overwhelmed by the unarguable reality of them. The sheer force of it. A deep presence in his soul, that was them. He was a family man. He would never deny them. He couldn't. It was physically impossible for him to deny them. The vice-principal, a deeply caring woman who'd given her life and everything else to her students and her staff, when he had confided in her in a moment of weakness, had placed her hand on his shoulder and said, 'You are not enough of a bastard, Andy, to ever be a great success as an artist.' Was it true? It stabbed him in the heart to hear her say it.

Lang said, 'I have an idea that might be the answer for both of us.'

Andy took another drink. Lang's wine was grim stuff. 'The answer to what?'

Lang was watching him. 'I've been staying with Sergei in Ballarat. I got home last week. He brought me a bag of groceries tonight.' He drew on his cigarette. 'I've decided to pretend to have a nervous breakdown.' He looked at Andy. 'You know that phys ed teacher . . . what was her name?'

'Carol.'

'Carol. She faked a nervous breakdown and got out on an education department pension. A full pension for life!'

'You're going to do that?'

'I'm only on temporary leave at the moment. Carol made her escape from the trap. I'm working on it. If I were free I could do the rounds of all the suburban auctions. You and I could work together. We can pretend we don't know each other. I'll give you the nod when something worth having is coming up. You wouldn't need to teach anymore.'

Andy said, 'Carol was a nut case. Anyone who fakes a nervous breakdown is having a nervous breakdown.'

'I'm not having a breakdown.'

They sat in the silence, the air heavy with Lang's cigarette smoke and the smell of the cheap red wine. A slight tension between them now. The hiatus of their disagreement.

'I used to be able to buy interesting works at the suburban auctions. Not things for my collection, but things I could research and sell for a handy profit. It was more than pocket money. Odd pieces overlooked by the auctioneers and the dealers' scouts. Every now and then, once a year or so if I was lucky, I'd discover something worth keeping: a nice English drawing, or an old Dutch engraving. I found a small McCubbin oil. A lovely little thing. The ruins of a cottage overgrown by ivy. I remember it was the warm red of the bricks that alerted me to it. The lovely brushstrokes just visible through the dirt. Painted on a board. It was black with grime except for that telltale warmth of old brick pushing through the years of neglect. Maja Janos restored it for me. It came up beautifully with a clean and a bit of a touch-up here and there. We put it in an expensive gilt frame and sold it through one of the big auction houses. I should have kept it and said nothing about it. I can't do that anymore. Nowadays they all know me. The dealers' scouts have been told to bid me up as soon as I show a bit of interest in something. They keep going till I have to pull out. I can't compete with them.' He refilled his tumbler and took a drink then sat gazing at Andy. 'Have you sold any more of your stories? I liked that story you showed me about the man who shot wild horses for a living. I still see it. It was very vivid.'

'He would have shot your mother cat.'

'I believe you. He was without empathy.'

'I haven't done any writing.'

'So there. You need to get out or you'll never write.'

Andy smiled.

'Last time I saw you, you said if you didn't have to teach for half the week, you'd be able to keep your writing front and centre of your mind and that would improve the quality of what you were doing. Do you remember saying that? Do you still feel like that?'

'I was just talking.'

'You've got a good eye, thanks to your father. You know what you're looking at. The amateur stuff doesn't fool you.'

'My father was an amateur. He didn't seek distinction. Art was his private world.'

'You could bid for me. That's what I'm saying. No one in the art trade here knows you. Most of these people don't know anything about art. They don't know what they're looking at. They need a signature and provenance. They don't trust their eye. With my help you could make enough money to give up teaching.'

'And become a dealer?'

'No, no, not a dealer. No. You could help me and help yourself. That's all. You'd enjoy it. I'll introduce you to Maja Janos. She's the best there is. She trained in Budapest and then in Paris with the greatest restorers.' He kept looking at Andy, considering him, making a judgement. 'You'd get on with Maja. She'd like you. She'd see the best in you.' Lang laughed. He was suddenly caught by a spasm of coughing, a thick, phlegmy cough that left him wheezing and out of breath. He breathed with difficulty and took a long drink. Then he lit a fresh cigarette and inhaled deeply. 'What do you think?' His voice was hoarse. 'Is it worth thinking about?'

'It's an idea, I suppose.'

'Would Jo object?'

'Probably.' Andy grinned. 'She thinks you're a bad influence.'

'Lucky she's not your mother then.' Lang glanced at him, assessing Andy's reaction to this remark.

Andy was thinking that Lang looked older. He took a drink. 'I'm not complaining,' he said. 'I've got nothing to complain about.' He looked hard at Lang. The vastness of his failure was the legend of his life. The thought came to Andy then that sooner or later the totality of Lang's failure was surely going to kill him. Wasn't that what always happened to the hero at the end of the legend? The death of the hero. It was a title. For the present, he was still living it. For now, it was enough to have a dragon on his roof and the hope in his heart that one day his love would return to him and he would once again become the master of his gift rather than its victim.

In a quietly interior voice, as if he'd only half intended to speak the thought aloud, Lang said, 'The galleries and the big auction houses trust me. Everyone knows me. They all trust me. When they're unsure of an Australian picture they get me to authenticate the work for them. They don't trust their own eye. It is my eye they trust. They know I never deal. They know my opinion is never double-edged.' He looked up at Andy. 'I'm trusted. I've earned it. I've worked for it. I have created this position of trust for myself among the dealers and the auctioneers. They are not people who offer their trust lightly. The trust I have earned from them is a big achievement.' He turned suddenly and looked towards the window. 'Did you hear that?'

'Hear what?'

'She has to fight off the tom cats. She has to conserve her strength for the kittens, but the toms won't leave her in peace.' He was silent awhile, listening. 'I go outside and the toms run off. She lets me know when I'm needed.' He listened a moment longer then turned to Andy. 'If I were to begin dealing, I would lose their trust.'

'So what's in it for you? Advising them, I mean?'

'They know what I collect and they put pictures my way. Do you want to sit in here or would you rather we went up to the front room? I can put the gas heater on up there.'

'I'm fine here.'

They sat for a while.

Lang said, 'You are my only true friend.'

Andy looked at him.

'I wouldn't trust anyone else to bid for me. I wouldn't ask anyone else to do that.'

'What about Sergei?'

Lang made a scoffing noise through his nose. 'Sergei in particular. Once people know you are dealing, they will never trust you again.' He refilled his tumbler and lit a fresh cigarette. 'I should go and check on her.' He didn't get up. 'I have always wanted to go to France and England to see the best of it. I have never been to Europe. It is one of the greatest regrets of my life. Now I have only one ambition left. It has long been my dream to own one of Sickert's nudes. Painted against the light. *Contre-jour*, the French say, and so we say it too, as they have the authority in such things. Literally, of course, it means against the day. Which I like. I always think: *against the day of my death*. His nudes are heavy with the suggestion of violence and disorder. I have always found them unsettling and seductive. Against the light. But how can a work of art be against the element of its own existence? To deny the light is to deny art. Is this why so many artists have felt compelled to paint black squares, as a statement of the impossibility of what they are attempting?' He drew on his cigarette and gazed before him. 'When all you can see is darkness, close your eyes.'

Andy saw how affected Lang was by the vast quantity of alcohol he'd drunk. How deeply happy he was at that moment. Fleetingly. The way happiness is. Like the approval of a beautiful stranger, to fade and be withdrawn as mysteriously as it is bestowed. Lang was handsome when he smiled.

'She will crown my collection. She will satisfy me. I've told you all this before. When I see her on my bedroom wall I will stop collecting. When I have the Sickert, I will know it is over.' After saying this, he drank then drew on his cigarette and said regretfully, 'But I'll never have the money for it.'

Andy said, 'Couldn't you sell some pictures from your collection to raise the cash?'

'That would make the whole thing meaningless.' Lang said this without feeling. As if it were an observed fact. 'I'd been drinking alone all day and far into the night. It was the tenth anniversary of losing her. In the early hours of the morning I went into my studio. I had decided to keep only those works I could still be proud of. One by one I went through the piles of gouaches and watercolours and the countless sketchbooks I'd filled over the years, and one by one I saw that each of them was an example of my failure to find the indescribable expressive capacity which I had found with my portrait of her. And one by one I tossed them aside into a pile on the floor of the studio. I knew that expressive capacity was attainable, because I had attained it by some miracle, painting her from my haunted memory, spurred on by the pain and love that was in me and which had found no release through the years with her. I found not her likeness, but her presence. Even now, when I look at that painting, it is her presence I see. When I came to look at the oil paintings I had kept, had even hoarded, you might say, and there were hundreds of them, I found the same deficiency that condemned the drawings and watercolours in my eyes. After I had finished going through my life's work, I saw with an honesty and clarity of vision that I was a failure. Yet I felt light. A load lifted off me. I was elated as I carried my works out into the garden, armful after armful, paintings and drawings and countless notebooks. I burned them all in a great fire that smouldered for two days and left a naked scar in the grass where to this day even thistles and docks don't grow.'

He reached for his tumbler and drank thirstily till it was empty, then he refilled it and looked at Andy and smiled. 'Did I tell you my portrait of Agatha was shortlisted for the Crouch Prize? I told you. Yes, I told you. Everyone said I should have won. Several weeks after the prize was announced I was drinking at the Royal Oak in Ballarat when a friend of one of the judges came into the bar. He came over and said he wanted to shout me a beer. We stood together at the bar drinking steadily and passing the time of day. When he was a bit loosened up, he said, *You should have won the Crouch*. I didn't say anything to this but waited, as I could see he was keen to get the thing off his chest. I remember he looked at me and said, *Them bloody judges were piss-weak, mate. We all knew it.* I was surprised to hear him say this as I knew he was a friend of the president or the chairman or whatever he was. He said, *They weren't prepared to give their precious bloody award to a Chinaman. Simple as that! They were never going to let a Chinese represent the Australian culture they'd dedicated their lives to promoting. It doesn't matter how long you Chinks have lived here*, he said. *It was just not on!*

'Well, I think I knew all that anyway. The Asian menace to the Anglo culture wasn't new to me. I'd lived my life under the White Australia policy. I knew all about it, and the fear of Chinese that went along with it. But no one had actually said it to me straight to my face the way he did. Had I won that prize, had those judges awarded it to Agatha's portrait, as they should have, I believe my life would have followed a very different path. I knew my portrait of Agatha expressed something of the best that was in me, the best that was in all of us. Others saw this too and claimed it for me loudly. I mean other artists, who are not always the most generous people to ask about the work of other artists, they said it. Two of them openly disputed the decision of the judges in the newspaper. As it was, that shortlisting turned out to be the high point of my career. It took a long time for me to accept this, but in the end I had to admit it. And I was forced to examine my own work and, when I did, I judged it harshly. No one judges our work more harshly than we do ourselves.' He drank off the wine remaining in his tumbler and suddenly stood up. 'It's all true. I'll show you the dead patch in the garden. Do you want to see it?'

Andy followed him out into the back garden. Ten or fifteen metres beyond the dying pear tree, where Agatha had sat reading her French novels on sunny days, there was a bare circle among the rank weeds and grass. It reminded Andy at once of places in the bush where a beast had perished, a cow or a heifer, or some old wandering bull. Whenever he and his boss were driving a mob of cattle through the bush and came on one of these sites, the cows would gather around and paw the ground and bellow in a way that was clearly a demonstration of mourning, a low moaning coming right up from deep inside them and the agitation of their movements. The minute Andy saw that dead circle on the ground in Lang's garden he thought of those cows moaning and bellowing, and he knew that circle was the site where Lang still mourned the death of art in himself, his momentous decision to accept the judges' verdict. The empty circle of his dreams. The night he gave up the struggle to find again that *indescribable expressive capacity* that he had found when he painted Agatha's portrait. It was the site where he had abandoned his attempt to make an Australian artist of himself, to render his work representative of Australian culture. The Crouch Prize judges had behaved as if that culture were something determined by the views and the aesthetics of their own generation, all descendants, one way or another, of British and European migrants themselves, all with their gaze fixed firmly on Europe as their guide and their ideal.

Listening to Lang, Andy understood for the first time, as they stood beside each other at the edge of the empty circle, that failure, all failure, becomes a person's reality the moment they cease to struggle. It was simple and it was real. He noticed, as he stood there next to Lang, looking at the barren section of soil, that at the edges of the circle a few small remnants of unburnt canvas had somehow survived the flames. He bent down and attempted to pick up a piece. It disintegrated softly between his fingers. It was, after all, only the imprint of unburnt canvas where the real substance of the canvas had rotted long ago.

They stood there, the two friends, side by side in the quiet garden, the pair of them saying nothing, knowing something deep and private had been shared between them. Andy understood that Lang was still mourning his past, that he was still vulnerable to his defeat, his failure to fight back and to persist while he'd had the energy to do so. He had given up while still believing in his heart that he possessed the gift that would make his work great one day, long after the culture those judges had spent their lives dreaming had become a brief moment in history.

Andy turned to look at Lang, the silhouette of his features against the light from the kitchen door.

Lang lit a cigarette. 'What is it?'

'Do you know for sure Agatha didn't go on with her art?'

Lang chuckled. 'You're right to ask. And the answer is no, how can I be sure? I have always had the feeling she went back to her father's country.'

'To France?'

'Her father came from Bordeaux. She insisted that Bordeaux was a unique place and was not really France. I believe she needed to answer the question in herself of what it meant to belong somewhere. I believe that was part of her quest.' He shrugged his shoulders. 'But who knows? I may be wrong. She could be anywhere. She could be still living in Melbourne. But I know she is not dead.'

'How do you know it?'

'I know it in my heart.'

'You still love her.'

'If you love someone, you love them forever.'

They were both silent. The night garden still and quiet. Then suddenly the mewling of a cat nearby. Lang said, 'See! She's asking me to feed her! Let's go in. I've got something for her. I asked at the shop. They said tins were best.'

They went back into the kitchen. Andy watched Lang open a small round tin of cat food. When Lang came back from placing the food on the bricks outside the back door he stood at the window. 'She's still shy. She'll come out in a minute. She knows you're here.'

Andy waited a while with him, but the cat didn't show up. He said, 'I have to go. Jo's on her own with Hennie.'

Lang said, 'Here she comes!'

Andy turned back to the window. A thin tabby cat came out of the grass and approached the tin of food. It stopped and looked up at the window.

Lang said, 'She's thanking me. See her eyes!'

They watched the cat eating the contents of the tin hungrily.

Andy said, 'I'd better get going.'

Lang didn't protest but went with him to the front door.

Andy said, 'Jo wants to meet you. She told me to invite you over for dinner.'

'That's very kind of her. Perhaps I can let you know when I'll be able to come.'

Andy said firmly, 'This coming Saturday, Lang. Jo told me to tell you she'll be offended if you don't come.'

'Would she really be offended?'

'No. Of course not. She'd be puzzled and disappointed. She wants to meet you. You're a bit of a mystery for her. If you don't come, she'll wonder what the problem is.'

'Please thank Jo for me,' Lang said, suddenly formal. 'And do please tell her I am looking forward very much to meeting her.'

Andy turned and looked at Lang. Lang's shoulders might have been those of a young boy, their narrow shape beneath the thin fabric of his fawn cotton shirt.

The shadows of the two men standing in the doorway, the strong light behind them, were cast out onto the wild grass and weeds of the front garden. Caught in the light was a single rose, white on its leafless bush.

Andy left him there. The night sky was streaked with red and yellow layers of cloud against a deep purple. In the car, Andy was thinking of Lang going back to his cask of bitter wine. As if he were going back to his lover. Maybe standing by the kitchen window meeting the trusting gaze of the mother cat. Andy remembered then visiting his father in England when his father was old. They sat together by the fire in the flat. His father said, 'Old age, after all, hasn't made me angry. I thought it would.' And he had looked at Andy and smiled. 'Old age is sad, that's what it is.' It was the last time Andy saw his father alive.

12

Monday morning, Jo had gone off to work earlier and Andy was sitting at the green garden table outside the back door writing in an old school notebook. A soft breeze found its way into the narrow space of the garden every now and then, softly lifting the edges of the pages. Hennie was lying in her bouncer on the table beside him. She was wide awake, her fingers occupied with the dangling things hanging from the bouncer's canopy. He had decided earlier not to take her to the creche. It was a beautiful day and she was in such a calm mood, he had wanted to enjoy being with her in the peace and quiet of the morning, just the pair of them together in the sunny back garden. It calmed him to be near her when she was in this mood. As he wrote he was aware of her making gurgling sounds, the sounds of contentment.

He had begun writing up his notes on Lang with an account of their first meeting.

> *That morning I walked into the staffroom and saw him standing there smoking and looking exotic and interesting. Off with the fairies, my mother would say. He had the classic look of the dreaming loner. I immediately wanted to get to know him.*

Elaborating the detail of his memory of that morning was an effortless pleasure. He had not asked himself how he should go about writing the memory, he had simply begun to write it. There was in this act of writing no expectation of distinction, so there was also none of the usual anxiety that he associated with writing his fictions whenever he went into the study and sat at his desk in front of his typewriter. Out here in the garden with Hennie and the notebook there were no self-conscious decisions about style, or whether to write the account in the first person or the third. He had begun to write with the innocence of his father's art, the solitariness of it, its privacy, and had soon become lost to the passing of time.

On the cover of the notebook he had written in block capitals: *SOME NOTES ON MEETINGS WITH A FRIEND.*

He numbered the pages but didn't put his own name in the book. There was no need. He wasn't claiming authorship. No potential reader or publisher was looking over his shoulder assessing his performance. It was the first time he had ever written with such ease, without the anxiety of being judged. He didn't ask himself if he was getting it right, he just wrote the words that came into his head.

He realised Hennie had gone to sleep. He should have changed her. He wasn't going to wake her up to do it now. When she woke, then he would heat up one of the bottles of milk Jo had expressed earlier and put in the fridge. Hennie was easier to change when she was sucking on a bottle of her mother's milk. He stood up and stretched. His shoulders ached from the unaccustomed position. He looked at his watch. He'd been writing nonstop for over an hour. Fifteen pages and he was still with Lang in their first meeting. His surprise, and the gratification he'd felt, when Lang suggested they go to the pub together for lunch had blossomed into a reflection on first impressions, including his first impression of Jo when he was making his way along the aisle of the bus. What he saw then was a lovely young woman smiling at him, not as if she were particularly attracted to him or impressed by his appearance, but with a generous kind of amusement, as if she saw in him someone already familiar to her, as if his presence on the bus was not unexpected. There was a confidence in her welcoming smile that put him at ease with her at once. How these chance encounters had determined the direction of his life. Supposing he had not decided to take that bus trip to Sydney over the Easter break. He looked at the sleeping features of his daughter. 'You wouldn't exist, my darling. Where would either of us be today?'

He sat down now and took up where he'd left off, he and Lang walking back to the school together from the pub for their afternoon classes. Had he made a new friend? He wanted to trust the truth of it. The hope of it. For Lang to see himself now as a failed artist, he must once have had public ambitions for his art and his reputation, the ordinary desire for distinction and success that Andy's father had not been troubled by.

When Hennie woke later, Andy saw that he had written thirty pages. He had still not finished dealing with the first meeting. He was going to need a new notebook. He stood looking down at the closed notebook on the table. Then he leaned over and wrote a large 1 on the cover. He would go on with it later. First to feed and change Hennie. The sun was still shining, so he'd take her down to the supermarket and get something for dinner. And maybe go on down and take a look at the bay. The breeze would be stronger out on the water, and there were sure to be sailing boats on a day like this.

* * *

That evening Andy and Jo were sitting in their regular positions on the couch after doing the washing-up. They were drinking a last cup of tea for the day. This had become a necessary ritual for Jo since she'd given up drinking alcohol for Hennie's sake. The television was on but they were watching Hennie. She was lying on her pink blanket on the floor, sucking a bit of the blanket she'd got hold of. Every now and then she lost the blanket and flailed around for a while before she got hold of it again. She blinked rapidly when she retrieved the corner of blanket and got it between her gums. A great achievement, evidently.

'She's a genius,' Andy said.

'Of course. What else did you expect?' Jo looked into the fire. 'I'll make my chicken pie.'

'You always get anxious about getting the pastry right.'

'Then I do get it right. Don't I?'

'You do. Yes. For sure. I'm not saying you don't get it right.' He took a sip of tea. 'Lang said he couldn't remember the last time he'd been invited to dinner.'

'Did you believe him?'

'Why would he say it if it wasn't true?'

'From what you've told me, he likes to fantasise about his life. You said he sees himself as a culturally dislocated person. Someone isolated. Not having a social life would be part of that image, wouldn't it? It sounds as if being seen as an isolated loner is important to him.'

'I just didn't think to doubt him.'

'You trust people too readily.' She cuddled up to Andy, resting her head against him. 'Put your arm around me.'

He put his arm around her and held her against him. She was warm. 'I think Lang trusts me.'

She murmured something, then said more clearly, 'Maybe he just needs you. It sounds as if no one else he knows would bid for him at the auctions.'

'Who knows? Maybe I'll find a bargain for us to go above the fireplace while I'm at it.'

'That would be good. You might come across some interesting books too. Does Lang have a library? I'd be interested to see it if so. Armand says people's books reveal more about them than their pictures.'

Andy wondered if this were true. 'Armand would say that, wouldn't he? I've seen a few art books, but it's mostly auction catalogues lying around in the kitchen. There aren't any bookshelves in the living rooms.'

Jo said, 'Look! She's gone to sleep. Turn that thing off and let's go up to bed.'

In bed, after settling Hennie, Andy and Jo made love. Neither of them was sleepy afterwards. This was not as it had once been. Jo had always gone straight to sleep after making love. Neither of them said anything about the fact that they were both lying there wide awake instead of sleeping in each other's arms, but the truth was that making love had been disappointing. It had felt, for both of them, as if they were determined to reassure each other that they'd got back to how it had been before Hennie. But the original fierceness of desire was not there. Sex didn't have the same urgency now.

Andy was trying to convince himself that it was because Jo and he were still coming to terms with the enormous changes Hennie had brought into their lives, one of which was that they no longer had a lot of spare time to simply enjoy each other's company, and maybe they were just tired these days. Andy hoped things would soon settle down and they'd find the original intensity again. But he couldn't help fearing that Hennie's massive reality, the constant pressure of need from her, had shifted them into a new place. He was worried the shift might be permanent.

Jo said into the silence, 'Armand has given me sole responsibility for seeing Margaret Symonds's letters into print.'

'Yes, you told me. That's wonderful, darling. You'll be running his business for him one of these days. How are you going with the project?'

'I think about it all the time. The letters are from a woman who lived on a pastoral property in the Western District during the late nineteenth century. Her family were sheep breeders in Dumfriesshire in Scotland. They kept her letters.'

'So how did Armand get hold of them?' Although there were no lights on in the bedroom, it wasn't really dark. A lot of light was reflected in from the street. Even the changing colours of the traffic lights at the corner were visible on the ceiling. He had never noticed this before. Once he had noticed it, he found it difficult not to go on watching the regularity of the change.

'The collection came up for auction in Edinburgh ten years ago. One of Armand's contacts over there alerted him to the letters and he bought them. They've never been published, so this isn't strictly a reprint. He said it was having me working there with them that decided him and Diana now was the time to publish them.' She glanced at him. 'You don't seem very interested.'

'Sorry. No, of course I'm interested. You know I am.'

She said nothing to this.

He found himself watching the reflections on the ceiling of the changes of the traffic lights again.

Jo said, 'I suppose Agatha may have left Lang because she saw there wasn't going to be any room for her own struggle in a life with someone as self-obsessed as him.'

This had never occurred to Andy. He said, 'Who knows?'

Jo murmured, 'What's the point of saying anything?' She sighed and turned over.

He wondered what the problem was.

Jo had always gone to sleep more easily than him. He had thought this might change once she was waking in the night to feed Hennie, but it hadn't. After feeding Hennie and putting her down in her cot, Jo still went to sleep again at once, her breathing deep and steady, giving out a snore or two only seconds after being wide awake. There was no way Andy could ever do that. Sleep was elusive for him. He envied Jo her sleeping ability.

Lying awake with Jo snoring steadily beside him, Hennie silent, the thought came to him that if Jo was right about Agatha's reason for leaving Lang, then Lang's account of Agatha's self-isolation might also not be trustworthy. It was Jo's suggestion that Lang was inventing things about himself to bolster his image as a disconnected man, living the image of the romantic artist who has failed because he is an outsider to some kind of master system of the culture in which he lives, rather than failing simply because he hasn't persisted against the odds. Weren't all artists outsiders?

Hennie was making strange noises. He got out of bed and went around to check on her. She was lying on her back, her eyes wide open, enthralled by the shifting patterns of light on the ceiling. The strange sounds were her talking to herself, quiet, calm and interior, a private language of her own, the pre-language of burbles. She didn't seem to be aware of him. He was spying on her. Watching her in her private moment. A half-memory came to him, not a real memory, but a sense of something that had once been his own private reality as a baby, before he could speak or walk. And he understood, that he had known at that time that he was fully himself and that he stood at the centre of it all, that he *was* the centre of it all. Hennie, he understood then really for the first time, was not coming into being but was already a whole person with her own world. She was fully here. Her eyes shone with intelligence and curiosity in the shift of reflected light from the street, the beams of passing vehicle headlights sweeping across the blank white plaster as if they were signs portending change.

He stood at the end of their bed watching Jo sleeping. Her lips twitched every few seconds and she made small snuffling sounds. Was the memory of Hennie still inside her? The womb's memory of its first child? What must that feel like? Being empty again? Surely the womb would soon begin to develop a hunger to be filled once more, to be *with* child instead of without child? The womb's purpose, after all, was to bring new life into the world.

13

Andy was on the phone to the school coordinator on Saturday evening when Lang knocked at the front door. Andy covered the phone with his hand and yelled, 'Can you get it, darling?'

Jo carried Hennie past him and opened the door. Andy heard her greet Lang. She took him through to the kitchen. Andy resented being called by the school at seven on a Saturday evening. The coordinator had apologised and said in a tired and aggrieved tone of voice, 'I'm sorry, but I really don't have any other free time, Andy.'

She was trying to convince him to work on Monday mornings so that he could attend their weekly staff meetings, which were held before classes started on Mondays.

'I have to be honest with you, Andy—not being available for the meetings has made you unpopular with the full-time staff and particularly with the ones responsible for things like timetabling and coordination. You don't have any extra responsibilities.'

Andy was well aware that not being at the Monday meetings, and hardly ever reading the memos and handouts that were circulated regularly, put him out of touch with what the other teachers were doing. They were mostly young people, eager and ambitious to do well. To make their mark. To be professional. He was avoiding becoming an active member of their community and he knew he was resented for it.

Andy said, 'Now that Jo's working again, I have to take our daughter to the creche on Monday mornings and I pick her up again at lunchtime. We've just got our system worked out.'

Diedre's voice was loud and insistent. He was sure she had been drinking. It was hard for him to get a word in. Diedre didn't tolerate being interrupted when she was sober. Andy was anxious to know how Jo was getting on with Lang in the kitchen and he finally cut in on Diedre. 'I can't do it, Diedre! Okay? I'm telling you Monday mornings are out. It's just not possible.' He was forced to raise his voice. He was being determined and letting his irritation show.

There was a long silence. Just the sound of heavy breathing from her end. Then she came out with it. 'You're so fucking special, Andrew Mc-fucking-Pherson! Oh my God! What is it with you people? An un-fucking-published genius!' She was yelling now, letting it out. She was shouting so loudly he was forced to hold the phone away from his ear. She was really cracking the shits now.

'We have good people here, Mr Mc-fucking-Pherson! People who put their guts on the table for the likes of you! They're working their arses off every fucking weekend while you sit at home writing your unpublished shit. Who the living fuck do you think you are? Franz fucking Kafka?' She gave a gulping sob and smashed the phone down.

He laid the phone gently in its cradle and stood a moment, gathering himself. His first thought was of having to face up to her when he went in on Wednesday afternoon. He was shaken.

He walked slowly back down the passage and on through to the dining room. He was feeling a kind of inward shattering from that shrieking voice aimed into his ear, the venom in it. There was the possibility, after all, that what Diedre said was true. He felt resentful for feeling guilty and doubting himself. Maybe he really was a self-obsessed mediocrity. Her world was not his world. Being an unpublished writer wasn't the easiest thing to be. Did she know that?

The truth was, he hated the school and the necessity of working there and being forced to deal with people like Diedre. Even admitting such people existed pained him. Apart from Lang, he had dismissed the lot of them as a bunch of nonentities. And they probably knew this. He couldn't stand their petty little hierarchies, like who was teaching senior students and who was teaching the lower grades. It was a caste system they lived by, possessive and narrow. And their endless meetings! Sacred enclaves, were they? Electing a new pope, was that it?

When he came into the kitchen he was surprised to see Lang sitting on the chair by the back door with Hennie on his lap. Lang's hair had no grey in it, but was still pure black and glossy. Lang was looking down at Hennie and she was looking back up at him. Each of them absorbed in the strangeness of the other. Was she the first baby he had seen up close? Or had these two known each other in a previous life? Lang looked at him.

'Diedre,' Andy said. 'How come she doesn't bug you about not being at meetings?'

'Diedre's not so bad,' Lang said. 'She likes a drink. We share a glass or two every now and then.' He grinned. 'You should ask her to lunch.'

'I'd rather shoot myself.'

Jo was at the bench preparing the strawberries, an open bottle of wine on the bench beside her. Andy poured a glass for himself and took a drink. Jo was wearing a white blouse, a shirt really, the sleeves rolled up, and her old denim skirt, which he loved. She turned to him and smiled. Her smile became a playful frown when she saw his expression. 'What? Are you okay, darling?'

He turned to face the back door. 'Look at those two!'

Jo said, 'They're lovers.'

Lang looked up. There were tears in his eyes. He smiled slowly. 'I think she's wet herself.'

Jo laughed and went over and took Hennie from him. She stood holding the child and looking down at Lang. He said, 'Thank you, Jo.'

'She loves you,' Jo said. 'Anyone can see that.'

He said, 'I don't think she has had time to get to know me.'

'Babies don't make a meal of things like love the way we do. They just follow their instincts.'

'Do you think so?'

'I know it.'

His gaze rested on Hennie.

Jo said, 'Have you seen the wild mother's kittens yet?'

'She hasn't brought them out. She is still cautious with me.'

'She'll bring them out and show them to you once they are weaned.'

'Do you think she will?'

'Did your friend Sergei really offer to shoot her?'

'He wanted to. I told him I would do it myself.'

'But you won't, will you?'

'No, I could not do that.'

She took one hand from Hennie and laid it on Lang's slim shoulder. 'I'll take her up and change her. She'll probably go down for a sleep after her feed. You can come up and have a look at her sleeping, if you like.'

'Thank you.'

Jo said, 'Will you finish this, darling? I shan't be long. They're nearly done.' She carried Hennie off and went upstairs with her.

Lang said, 'If I had what you have . . .' He broke off, moved, and reached for his wineglass and drank from it.

Andy said, 'You told Jo about your mother cat?'

'Your little daughter looks just like you.'

'A couple of people have said that. I don't see it.'

'She has your generous mouth.'

'I have a generous mouth? You could tell Diedre that.'

The Greek music had started up next door. The woman was singing along with it. She had a lovely mellow voice. The song was romantic and distant, of an age of adventure or suffering, a kind of lamentation with a story attached to it.

Andy turned and looked at Lang. He raised his glass. 'Here's to us!'

Lang met his gaze and he too raised his glass. 'To friendship!' He drank and set his glass on the bench. 'Will Jo mind if I smoke?'

'Jo will make an exception for you. Did Agatha smoke French cigarettes?'

'Agatha? She rolled her own.' At the mention of Agatha, Lang seemed to withdraw into his own sadness, along with the Greek music.

Andy went on topping and slicing the strawberries.

When Jo came back they moved into the dining room and Jo served up the chicken pie. The pastry had turned out fine. She was proud of it. The big round pie with the pastry knot on top, golden brown and heavy in the white dish. 'Help yourself to the vegetables, Lang.'

He thanked her. Andy felt he was pretending to like the food. The mood between them was flat while they ate. Lang had little to say.

Andy made coffee after the strawberries. Lang said he didn't drink coffee. He looked at Jo and said, 'That was a very good pie, Jo. Thank you.' He turned to Andy. 'Could you call me a cab, please, Andy?'

'Sure. Of course.' Andy set down his coffee cup and went to the phone and called a cab. He asked them to tell the driver to give a blast on his horn when he was outside. He was puzzled by Lang's sudden withdrawal into himself. Throughout the dinner he had sensed the other man's longing to be alone. He was dismayed by the evening's failure.

In bed later, Jo said, 'Was it us? Or was it Lang? It started so beautifully with him falling in love with Hennie.'

'He seemed to be more at ease with you, in some ways, than he has ever been with me.'

'He needs something from you. He doesn't need anything from me. He's on guard with you. I noticed that.'

'You weren't there when I asked him if Agatha had smoked French cigarettes. He said she rolled her own and then seemed to withdraw into himself. I have to admit that often I just don't know where he's coming from.'

They fell silent. The sound of the odd car still going past along the road out the front, the sound coming through the side window, which they'd left open. The night was warm and still. A yell from some crazy drunk over at the flats every now and then punctuating the night.

Andy said, 'I think he found our domestic set-up here a bit depressing. I thought he was putting on an act. Trying too hard. And fucking glad to escape when the taxi came and rescued him.'

Jo said nothing. Andy turned his head and looked at her. She was asleep. He lay there wide awake for a long time, listening to the night sounds, a voice raised in anger or dismay across the road. He found himself thinking about his second notebook, his notes on his second encounter with Lang. He had filled the forty pages of the first notebook with their first meeting. He was rehearsing it in his mind. The words were there, waiting to be written down. He had never really looked forward to writing before this, but had always felt anxious about it. This was different. With the notebook recollections he felt himself to be alone and safe, as if the writing were something private that no one else would ever see. Nothing was riding on it. He was reluctant even to let Jo read it, in case she should be tempted to suggest improvements or ideas, in which case he would lose the simplicity of it. Like his father before him with his gentle watercolours, Andy found a freedom in the unquestioning innocence of the occupation of the note-making of his recollections. It was this he treasured. It was this, he understood, that might enable him to redeem himself from doubt. And perhaps one day he would be able to tell his father's ghost that he had found his way at last.

14

The following morning, after dropping Hennie off at the creche, Andy drove across town to Richmond. He parked in a side street and walked around to Sullivans. It was a barn of a place, the front room filled with old furniture from deceased estates, with junk spilling out onto the footpath. Inside, shifty-looking men and nervous young people looking to furnish their place cheaply were clustered around the auctioneer. He had already moved past the better pieces in the front room and had begun selling the less interesting things in the back room. The auctioneer's mate brought each item to the attention of the assembly before the auctioneer knocked it down to the and many of them were laid aside without attracting a bid. A box of old doorknobs was quickly followed by a carton of hinges and a torn canvas and one or two other odds and ends. When the auctioneer's mate indicated this lot with the toe of his boot, the auctioneer yelled out the number and Andy's hand shot up and he yelled back, 'Five dollars.' It was knocked down to him at once and the action moved on to the next item. Andy went out to the street, where he waited till the auction was over, then he went back in and paid his five dollars at the front desk and picked up the carton and carried it around to his car and put it on the back seat without examining its contents.

Andy locked the car and crossed the road. In the newsagency he bought three Spirax notebooks and a new Bic. He went into the pub next door and bought a beer and took it to a table on the street. He set his beer and the notebooks on the table and sat down and wrote a large 2 on the cover of one of the notebooks. He sat awhile, drinking his beer and watching the traffic and people on Bridge Road. Then he opened the notebook with the number two on the cover and began to write.

When he got back to his car later there was a parking ticket on the windscreen. He peeled it off and put it in his pocket. Driving home through the traffic he was happy.

* * *

At home Andy sat at his desk and opened the notebook with the 1 on the cover and began typing out his account of his first meeting with Lang. He had intended to copy it word for word, but as he re-entered the memory, elaborations of what he'd written came to him. He was lost in the reclamation of his memories when the door of his workroom opened and Jo put her head around it and looked in at him.

'Hi, you're back. What's going on?' She came into the room and stood by the desk and looked down at the open notebook. 'So you're writing?'

He closed the notebook and stood up. 'It's just a few notes. Lang and me and some thoughts about friendship. Maybe it's the beginning of something. I don't know. I'm not sure yet. I'll let you see it when it's done.'

She looked around the study then took a book off the shelf beside her. *John of Salisbury's Memoirs of the Papal Court*. Did you really read this?'

'We referred to it.'

'So how did you go at Sullivans?'

'I got it.'

'Where is it?'

'I left it in the car. I'll take it over later.'

'What's it like?'

'It's a crude painting of three men playing cards in a hut. One of them's Chinese. He wants me to pick up anything from the old days in Australia with a Chinese connection. Kind of proof, I suppose, that Chinese people lived normal lives here in the early days like everyone else.'

'Come and have a cup of tea. I made a plain seedcake. It's still warm.' She replaced John of Salisbury's *Historia pontificalis* on the shelf next to Eadmer's *Life of St Anselm*. Books that had sat unopened since 1964, when Andy finished reading Medieval History.

He followed her down the passage. In the kitchen she poured the tea and cut the cake. They sat at the kitchen table.

'This cake's brilliant.' Seedcake was his favourite.

'I made it for you.' She smiled, looking at him eagerly.

'You've got some news? What is it?'

She laughed. 'She walked.'

'Bullshit! Fair dinkum?'

'She dragged herself upright against the kitchen cupboard and stood. The look in her eyes was fierce. I knew she was going to take a step. She staggered across the kitchen to me and clutched my pants. Five steps! I held my breath! Before she walked she ate a whole bowl of mashed banana.'

He sipped his tea and took a second piece of cake and bit into it. 'Is she early?'

'Thirteen months is pretty average.'

'She's not average.'

'Of course not.'

'She's a genius. I can't wait to see her walk.'

When Andy pulled up outside Lang's house later that day, Lang was standing at his front door smoking. Andy grabbed the carton with the picture in it and stepped over the low wall into the garden. Lang came towards him and took the carton from him. 'Let's have a look!' Andy had never seen him so excited. Lang set the box down on the tiles of the porch and took out the forlorn old piece of canvas in its broken stretcher. He took the canvas back out into the garden and held it to the sunlight. The painting was crude. The work of an amateur. What the collectors and dealers called naive, the work of an untrained artist. On the art market, such a thing was of no value.

Lang poked his finger at the image. 'See!' he said, triumphant, as if the picture proved him right about something.

Andy looked over his shoulder. The small oil painting was of three men sitting on stumps around a table, playing cards. Behind them the open door to their hut, a rough representation of sunlit bush beyond the door.

Lang said, 'Three outsiders.'

One of the men had a long queue down his back and was depicted as Chinese. The one in the centre had red hair and a wild beard, and might have been a caricature of an Irishman. The third man was black. He was wearing the smart riding outfit of a gentleman, with high boots, tight breeches and a red coat. A handwritten title under the painting: *Euchre in the Bush*.

Andy said, 'Outsiders? Isn't the black guy an Aborigine?'

'He looks English or American to me. An outsider here *and* over there. What do you think?' Lang carried the picture into the house. In the kitchen he laid it on the table and studied it closely. He was delighted with it. 'How much did you pay for it?'

'Five dollars.'

'You could have got it for a dollar.'

'I didn't want to take the chance of losing it.'

Lang took out his wallet and held out a five-dollar note to Andy.

'Don't be silly!' Andy waved the money away.

Lang put the money back in his wallet and resumed studying the painting. He straightened up after a few minutes and shook an accusing finger at it. 'See! We've been here for eight generations, but we're still not Australians.' He looked at Andy. 'Why not?'

15

Late Saturday evening and Lang was standing up close to the gas fire in the sitting room at the front of his house. It was raining heavily, the rain rattling against the window, driven by sudden powerful gusts of wind. The angry storm had rolled across Melbourne earlier, barrelling in from the Southern Ocean, bringing an Antarctic chill with it. Lang was gripping a tumbler of the cheap cask wine in his hand and smoking a cigarette. He held the glass firmly, as if he feared it might slip from his hand. He was facing the portrait of Agatha, his eyes narrowed to slits, the smoke from his cigarette circling his head in the updraft from the rising warmth of the gas fire. He jabbed the cigarette at the portrait repeatedly, not quite touching its surface. Accusing the painting or the sitter, claiming it or claiming her, maybe. It was a gesture he made often, pointing his finger and shaking it and laughing at the same time, an expression of amused contempt, for himself or for everything. He gave his characteristic little chuckle and looked down at Andy, who was sitting cross-legged on the rug facing the gas fire. Andy was holding in his lap the crude painting of the shepherd's hut with the three men playing cards around a makeshift table. The painting had been cleaned and repaired and put into a new stretcher by the restorer, Maja Janos.

Andy felt Lang looking down at him and he looked up and met the other man's eyes. He could feel Lang wanting to say something. Lang was very drunk. It showed. He must have been drinking all day. He was swaying slightly, like an old person trying to maintain their balance. His eyes were almost completely shut. He said, 'So now you're getting pressure from three women.' His voice was heavy and hesitant. 'It's what happens to us. Either we give them pressure, or they give pressure to us. The pleasures of the middle way are fleeting.' He laughed, a richly phlegmy cough loose in his bronchi. He sighed heavily and took a deep drink from the tumbler in his hand, then sucked hard on the cigarette, as if he would defy by sheer willpower the thing that was working to defeat him.

Andy said, 'Diedre is making my life a misery. You know she said you're not one of us.'

Lang grinned. 'She was right.'

'I think she meant just different, as in you do your own thing. Until you asked me to buy this painting you had nothing Chinese in this house except that wooden box on the mantelpiece. Why the sudden interest in things Chinese?'

Lang hesitated, looking at the box as if startled to see it there. He slowly set his empty tumbler on the mantelpiece and reached for the box. He held it in both hands and gazed at it for a long time without saying anything. Andy saw that he had tears in his eyes.

'This is Berat's brush pot,' he said at last. 'They say I don't teach art and that I am just a childminder. But that's not true. That is all they see. Me and the kids out there in my art room. We don't give them any trouble, so they leave us alone. Berat was the most troublesome boy in the school. Small and intense, his will was set against the authorities. The bullies left him alone. If anyone looked sideways at him his reaction was severe. At first he was puzzled by me and my art room. He couldn't work out what was going on. There was nothing for him to kick against. He began coming over to my desk and watching me drawing with my brushes. One day he said, *Teach me to do that.*

'When I was a boy living with my mother and grandfather in my grandfather's old red mansion in Hangzhou, I was taught the art of the brush. My grandfather was a master. He had wanted a son so he could pass on his wisdom and his skills, but all he got was my mother. So he treated her as if she was his son and trained her in the discipline of the brush until she vied with the Hangzhou gentlemen who were both poet and painter, the great poet painters of those days. In a single eloquent stroke of her brush she could write a poem and paint a sacred landscape. She excelled in the discipline and made my grandfather proud. So then my mother taught me the art of the brush, stroke by stroke, until my soul was touched and the ink flew from my brush with a wilful flourish that delighted her.

'While I practised my art, my mother played the antique melodies on her zither, filling my grandfather's house with the ancient spirits. She had inherited the true music that calls to the old gods. So I gave Berat lessons. I have always taught any student who has asked to be taught; the others I respect and leave alone to do with their time whatever is their choice. I don't inquire. Berat was a diligent student for the first time in his life. The harder he worked the more desperate he became to make up for lost time. His ambition was to master the brush, but of course this was not possible for him. He could not know the reason why, but I knew. And that is why I weep whenever I think of Berat. A wonderful young man who was doomed to fail. The day he was leaving the school, he came to see me one last time and he presented me with this brush pot. Which I have never used. The writing on the side is his. It says, *To my master, the gift of the pot.* He had made it in the woodwork classes. A special project.'

Andy said, 'So Berat was a romantic. One of us. I wonder where he is now.'

The rain rattled against the window and the wind moaned in the chimney. Lang said, 'When we no longer have the antique music of our ancestors, we have lost the soul of our art. In such silence as this, our art has no meaning and can never again call the old gods into our presence. Without our music we can only weep, or laugh.' And he laughed, a sudden shout of laughter that made Andy jump. It was the slightly mad laughter of his despair.

Who else do I know, Andy asked himself, *who would ever say such a thing? Without our music we can only weep.*

Lang refilled his tumbler and drank the wine, and he stood facing his wife's portrait in the rising heat from the gas fire and he smoked and drank and swayed and every now and then he laughed.

Andy felt woozy from the heat of the room and the effect of the wine. He set the painting on the floor beside him. 'I'd better get going. It's late.'

Lang said, 'Without our music we have nothing. You and I have lost everything. Berat had lost everything. Without our old gods our souls are empty. We are exiled from our meaning. It is how we live now. Our story ended a long time ago. We are people of the broken story.'

Andy struggled to his feet and went out to the toilet and took a piss. The bowl was stained with brown and the smell was of stale urine. The woman who came to dust the furniture and plump the cushions obviously didn't make it to the toilet or the bathroom. Andy was wishing he hadn't drunk so much. He could hear the mewling of the mother cat outside. He zipped up his fly and pulled the chain that hung from the old iron cistern. The cat sounded desperate, its cry pleading. He went out into the kitchen and opened the back door. A blast of cold air hit him. There was no sign of the cat. The wind thrashed wildly in the cotoneasters. Agatha's leafless tree trembled as the gusts shook its branches. He closed the door and went back up the passage and into the warmth of the front room.

Lang was lying on the floor. His tumbler of wine had rolled to the table by the window where the dead hydrangeas still waited in their crystal vase. The stain of the spilled wine was a slash of dark red across the pale carpet. Lang was curled into the foetal position. He was moaning. He called weakly, 'Help me, Andy.' The smell of shit was strong. Lang's bowels had emptied into his slacks. *Euchre in the Bush* was lying where Andy had left it. He bent and picked it up and placed it on the table next to the vase of dead hydrangea blooms.

Lang was weeping and moaning. Andy took him in his arms and carried him across the passage and into his cold bedroom. He was not heavy.

Andy laid him on the bed on his side and went down to the bathroom. He ran the hot water and wet one of the towels. He felt nauseated and very sober now. He was wondering if he should call an ambulance. It was after midnight. Outside, the cat was still mewling pathetically.

Back in Lang's bedroom, he stripped off Lang's slacks and pulled off his underpants. The mess was watery and had gone right down to his sock on his left foot. Andy pulled off both shoes and socks. He washed Lang clean. He could not believe he was doing it. He didn't mind. Lang's legs were very thin, his thighs hollow where the muscle should have been. His buttocks were almost non-existent, just the bony shape of his pelvis. Andy's mother would say there was nothing to him. She wouldn't be far wrong.

When Andy had finished cleaning Lang, he pulled back the bedclothes and rolled him into the bed then pulled the covers up. He put a hand to Lang's shoulder through the blanket. 'It's okay, Lang. Don't cry.' He patted the slight rounding of his shoulder. 'It's okay.' He stood looking down at him. 'I'll be back in a minute. I'll just take your stuff down to the bathroom. Your bedroom smells like a public toilet, old mate.'

Andy rolled the soiled clothes together and took them down to the bathroom and rinsed them in the sink before putting them in the old top-loading washing machine. His mother had had a similar model. One of the early twin tubs. Then he washed his hands thoroughly.

Before returning to the bedroom, Andy checked the fridge. There was an opened tin of cat food covered in clingwrap. He took it out and scooped some of the meat onto a saucer then opened the back door and put the saucer down on the bricks where Lang usually left it. The rain was still coming down. He went back inside and shut the door. He stood and waited. On the table among the catalogues there were a number of unopened brown envelopes. New catalogues from Christie's and Sotheby's in London. Within a minute the crazy mewling of the cat fell silent. He put the remainder of the tin back in the fridge.

He went out and down the passage. Jo would have given up waiting and be asleep by now. He stood by the phone in the hall then picked up the receiver and rang their number. Jo picked up after two rings.

'I thought you must have had an accident. Where are you?'

'Lang collapsed.'

'What do you mean, collapsed?'

'He collapsed. Lay on the floor moaning. He'd shat himself. I had to clean him up and put him to bed. I'll go in and have a look at him before I call an ambulance. I'll have to find out who his GP is.'

'You washed him? He'll feel humiliated.'

'I had to. What else could I do? I didn't really mind all that much.'

They were silent. Then she said, 'Give me a call once you know what you're doing.'

'I thought you'd be asleep.'

'I was worried about you. And Hennie's been restless. She feels a bit hot. I hope she's not coming down with something. I can't find the thermometer. You don't remember where you put it last time, I suppose?'

'I don't remember having it.'

'You had it. The clinic's not open on Sunday. Of course it would be Saturday night. I'll have to wait till Monday. The nurse doesn't get in till ten on Mondays. I'll give Diana a ring at home in the morning and let her know I'm going to be late on Monday. Are you sure you don't remember having the thermometer?'

'She might be teething.'

'She's not that sort of restless.'

They talked for a while longer. After the call Andy went back into Lang's bedroom. Lang was lying on his back. He turned his head and looked at Andy, an expression of fear in his eyes. 'I thought you'd left me!'

'I was talking to Jo. I fed the cat.' He stood by the bed looking down at Lang. 'Maybe I should call an ambulance. How are you feeling?'

Lang reached a hand out of the bed and took hold of Andy's hand. 'Don't call an ambulance. I'll be all right by the morning.' He was clinging firmly to Andy's hand. Clutching him. 'Don't tell anyone about this, will you? You are my only true friend, Andy.'

Andy thought Lang was going to start crying again. He sat on the side of the bed and patted Lang's hand. It was what his mother had done when he had measles. Patting the hand helped. He remembered it. It was a comforting gesture. A reassurance. It said all the things that couldn't be spoken. How alone Lang was! To say something like that: *You are my only true friend.* It would be terrible to be so alone in the world. And was he really Lang's friend? He wasn't even sure of that himself. How much was he prepared to do for Lang to help him get through this crisis? He thought of the words of the song 'Help Me Make It Through the Night'. He hadn't told Lang about the notebooks. He would write a detailed account of all this in his notebook in the morning.

He sat in the silence, holding Lang's hand. The wind rattling the window in its frame. 'What's your doctor's number? You'll need to talk to him.' The fingers of Lang's hand felt like the fingers of a child's hand, smooth and tender but with a surprising strength in them, a determination in the grip that said, *Don't let go of me!*

'I don't have a doctor. I've never been ill. If I need something, I have herbs. My mother and grandfather never saw Western doctors in their lives, except when my mother was pregnant with me. Then my father insisted. But Western medicine was never my mother's choice.' His voice trailed on, memories of his mother and the old red mansion of his boyhood in Hangzhou.

While Lang talked of his childhood home, Andy looked into the depths of the intricate pencil drawing of the tree fern gully on the wall above Lang's head. An old drawing from another time. The time of close attention to the details of nature, a search for the knowledge of those things distant from Europe. The eye of a European penetrating the Australian bush, going down into the cold shadows of the gully to locate its exotic secrets. The eye of the practised stranger.

Andy felt Lang's fingers relax. He looked at him. Lang was asleep. He didn't look ill. The face of a man asleep. Liberated from the anguish of living. Dreaming of China and home. Was it home for him? Did anyone in the modern world really have their ancestral home anymore? He thought of Lang's devoted attempt as a boy newly arrived in the school in Ballarat to make himself over into an Australian. Exhausted by his failure. Still Chinese. Sleeping alone. Andy slipped his hand out of Lang's grip. What was he going to do? Would Lang want him to get in touch with Sergei? Or maybe the woman who came to dust the furniture? Would she come on a Sunday morning? Probably not. Andy didn't even know her name. He had never met her. Lang kept them all apart, these separate segments of his life. A rumour from Maja of a brother in Canada, let slip in conversation. Did he really have a brother? Lang had told him he was an only child.

Sitting there on the side of the bed looking at his sleeping friend, Andy was thinking of the vast continent of his own ignorance about China. It was almost equalled by his ignorance of Lang's history, the story of his family, his origins and those things that still worked in him and made him who he had become. So he had secretly taught the few curious students something of the old art of the brush, the art that was both visual and literary. Another country altogether from the world of gentle English watercolours and Andy's own father's love of painting. Giving them a taste of a tradition that would never be theirs.

He went across the room and sat in the high-backed English chair that stood beside the chest of drawers. He was suddenly very tired. He would call Jo in a few minutes.

He woke to the sound of the front door slamming. A gust of cold air came into the room and flowed around his ankles. Daylight was filtering through the side of the curtains. Someone had come into the house, the whisper of footsteps across the hall.

He stood up and went out into the hallway.

The woman stopped and stared at him, startled by his presence. 'Oh!' she exclaimed. She was very short, heavy-set and about sixty years of age. Possibly Chinese. She was carrying a large red plastic bucket with cleaning materials sticking out of it.

Andy said, 'I'm sorry. I'm Lang's friend, Andy McPherson. We teach at the same school.' He half turned and gestured to the open bedroom door. 'He's had a collapse. I'm wondering if I should call an ambulance.'

The woman didn't appear to be worried about Lang. She said, 'I'll tell Tony to come.' She had a strong accent. She went over and picked up the telephone and dialled a number. She said a few words into the telephone in her own language then hung up. 'Tony is coming.' All this time she didn't look directly at Andy but looked past him or to one side of him, as if she addressed some other person, or she was thinking about something else. Or maybe she just didn't want to admit he was there.

She went through the glazed doors into the front room and began at once to work at the wine stain on the carpet.

Andy stood and watched her for a minute. She seemed utterly unperturbed by Lang's collapse. Her manner seemed to Andy to say, *So what? Why bother telling me?*

'Can you tell me who Tony is?' he asked.

She went on with her cleaning as if he hadn't spoken.

16

Ten days after Lang's collapse, Andy received a letter from him:

My dear friend,
Please forgive me! I have very little memory of that night, but I know I must have deeply embarrassed you. My apology also is to Jo. I hardly dare to think of you washing me and putting me to bed. Who else would have done this for me? There is no one. If Maria's husband Tony had not taken me straight to St V's that morning I don't know what we would have done. I am still deeply confused and shaken by what has happened to me. But the people here, particularly the social worker and the head doctor, are wonderfully kind. You will not understand, but for

a Chinese man the humiliation is insupportable. But these people encourage me and have given me a little faith that I may, with discipline and self-will, overcome my problem and once again find meaning in my life. That is such a remote possibility I find it difficult to believe in its reality. They have told me your friendship for me is critical to my recovery and will be a source of strength to me in this struggle. But now I am old and I ask myself, can I struggle again? I have struggled and failed and found a kind of contentment in my failure. Now I wonder if I can find the will and the energy to struggle yet again.

I try to believe them. I am resolved to try. I will be here for quite a while. I don't want to let them down. And I don't want to let you down. You also believe in me, as they do. I ask myself why this is. I have made a wreck of my life. Their humanity is deeply moving for me just as yours is. I trust them as I trust you. I have spent a lot of time weeping and thinking about my mother. I don't know what happened to her during the war. The doctor has told me that if I ever touch alcohol I will again lose control of my bowels. I could not live with that. My mother's shame, if she had lived to see me, would have been beyond even her fortitude to endure. I think of her all the time. It is as if her great spirit has reached out to me to offer comfort to my soul. Maria is feeding Mother Cat, so please don't worry about her.

Forgive me.

Lang

Andy didn't believe there was a need to reply to this letter. He even felt a bit relieved by Lang's temporary absence from his life. Guilty, but relieved. Knowing he was in good hands and recovering was a relief. Someone else had taken on the responsibility of looking after him.

Lang was released from the Alcoholism and Drug Dependence Unit at St Vincent's Hospital five weeks after being admitted. It was a warm sunny day. Andy had not seen Lang during his time in hospital, as visitors, except for close family members, were discouraged.

The first evening after Lang was released from the clinic, Andy and Jo were listening to the news in the kitchen. The announcer began by saying Mao had died of a heart attack. Fifteen minutes later the phone rang. Andy went out into the hall and picked it up.

Lang said, 'He's dead!'

They hadn't spoken since the night of Lang's collapse.

Andy said, 'You sound pleased.'

'Now I might be able to go back home to China.'

Andy felt a bit disappointed by the idea that Lang might be finished with his failure to become an Australian and had decided to call it quits and go home to China. Could China still possibly be his home? 'Do you want to go back to China?'

'I might be able to find out what happened to my mother.'

The way Lang said this was very moving. As if his search for his mother had been on hold all these decades, war and then Mao's so-called Cultural Revolution silencing China to him. Wrenched away from his mother and his familiar world in Hangzhou at the tender age of ten, the mystery of his mother's fate was still haunting Lang. Had haunted him all his life. He had made the best of his fate, a fate determined for him by his father, and had set out to become an Australian. It was obvious to Andy that Lang would have had about as much hope of becoming an Australian as Andy would have of becoming Chinese.

'You should also congratulate me,' Lang said. 'I've been granted a full disability pension by the department.'

'Congratulations!' he said. 'How was the clinic?'

'It was okay.' Lang sounded constrained, impersonal, cool even. 'I'm feeling a lot better, thank you.'

Andy wondered if this could be believed.

'And do you know what?' For a moment there was warmth and interest in his voice. 'Maria has coaxed Mother Cat into the house. She has become used to taking her food in the kitchen. She sleeps on one of my old blankets by the door and has her own litter tray.' He was silent for a few moments. 'The dietician at St V's also gave me a diet sheet that I have to follow. I will go to the Victoria Market on Saturdays and do my shopping. I must eat fresh vegetables and fruit.'

They were both silent. Andy felt as if he were talking to a stranger. Without wine, Lang sounded as if he was holding himself erect, holding himself upright against the weight of a reality that must sooner or later bring him down and crush the last hope out of him.

'I might be able to visit Hangzhou and see my grandfather's house.'

'Do you think it will still be there?'

'Not everything can have been destroyed. There must be records, at least.'

'After two generations of Communism you don't think maybe being Chinese will have come to mean something different from what it meant when you were a boy? Maybe everyone speaks Mandarin now. Maybe Communism has smoothed out the different cultures. You might not recognise the place.'

Lang gave a short scornful laugh. It was a real expression of amusement breaking free from the old familiar Lang. 'The Chinese will never change.'

Andy was a little reassured to hear it. Imagining Lang back in China, he was remembering an evening not long after he and Lang first met when Lang gave him his first lesson in what it might mean to be Chinese. Lang was buying takeaway Chinese in Brunswick Road after school. It surprised Andy when Lang spoke English to the man behind the counter, because the man behind the counter had spoken Chinese to his wife, who was there helping him. When they got outside Andy asked Lang, 'Why didn't you speak Chinese to that guy?' Lang said, 'I don't understand Cantonese. And he wouldn't understand Mandarin. French is closer to English than Cantonese is to Mandarin. Saying we're both Chinese doesn't mean any more than saying you and the Frenchman are both European. China is its own complicated world, just as Europe is. Because you all look European doesn't mean very much. It's not enough to understand one culture in order to understand China. There are many different cultures in China. You will never understand them all. That they have fought with each other and influenced each other at some point in their history doesn't make them the same any more than Germans and French have become the same over their centuries of conflict.'

After they'd hung up, Andy went back into the kitchen. 'That was Lang. He's out.'

'How is he?'

'He's sober. Flat. Full of facts. Are these cherries for something special?'

'Eat them!'

Andy grabbed a tea towel and started drying the dishes. 'He's not Lang anymore. They've changed him.'

'How do you mean?'

'He's playing a role he's been given by the clinic and he doesn't really believe in it but is determined to hang on to it. The old Lang is still there, but under the surface. He isn't really free to be himself anymore. It was upsetting. I felt like I was talking to a stranger. He's shut down his emotions in case the grog joins the party again. He's having to reinvent himself. He's talking about going back to Hangzhou where he grew up. It's almost as if he expects to find his mother still living there. But it's not just that; he doesn't *sound* like Lang.' Andy was eager to get to notebook number five while his recollection of the conversation with Lang was still sharp in his mind.

'I think Hennie might have picked up another bug at the creche. She was a bit hot and restless after I put her down.'

'I suppose we'll get it now.'

'We're sure to. She had a big day. Maybe she got overexcited. She ran to the swings today. You should have seen the look of mad glee in her eyes.'

'It's hard to get her away from those swings.'

Jo said, 'It sounds as if Lang has taken refuge in his memory of a more innocent past. Does he think he can reclaim his past in China and somehow pick it up and go on with it after all this time? Is that possible?'

'Probably not. A lot of migrants do go back to their old country.'

'And they nearly always come back here again.'

'Going home to Greece works for the Greeks. They keep in touch with their islands. They're here but they're still Greek. But for most people who return it just fucks up their life and they never find a home anywhere.'

'Have you ever thought of going back to England?'

'You must be joking! Home is here with you and Hennie. If it's fine Saturday we should take a picnic to the Botanic Gardens. She can run about on the grass. We could have lunch near the herb garden. It was always quiet there.'

'The Botanic Gardens,' Jo said, smiling. 'She was almost conceived there. Yes, let's do that after the market.'

17

Andy heard nothing more from Lang. It was into the third or fourth week that he decided Lang didn't really want him to visit. No doubt Lang was afraid of the drinking association between them. Andy missed sharing the circle of Lang's trust. The notebooks had become an absorbing project for him. Entering his memories of their meetings had surprised him. He had not foreseen how he would also be entering his memories of himself. In typing up the notes, new links offered themselves, and he saw that the thing was becoming a portrait not only of Lang but becoming of the difficult friendship itself. He loved doing it. Having no ambition for it, he had no fear of its failing.

Jo was keen to see what he was writing, but it was too soon to show her.

Andy and Jo were sitting on the couch, Hennie sprawled asleep between them. Jo had been telling him about her day at the bookshop. The evening was quiet and still, no mad drunks carrying on over at the flats, and no party at the Greeks' house next door. It was late when the phone rang.

When Andy made to get up to answer it, Jo put a hand on his arm. 'Leave it! It'll be him. I know it.'

They listened till the message machine cut in. Lang's tone was portentous. '*Fate, Andy, has begun to favour me at last. I have endured, and this is to be my reward.*' He paused, breathing into the phone. '*It is urgent, or I would not disturb you at this time of the evening. I need your help. Sullivans will auction it tomorrow morning. I have to grasp this opportunity. I can't tell you the details over the phone. You must come over. It doesn't matter what time you get here. I'll be waiting up for you.*' He hung up and the machine gave out its long beep, followed by silence.

Jo said, 'He's being a bit melodramatic, isn't he?' She looked at Andy steadily. 'You're not going over there *now*?'

'He's obviously found something at Sullivans and needs me to bid for him in the morning. If I'm going to do it, I'll have to go and get the details from him tonight. If I don't go over there now and he misses out on some old thing from China which might have forged a link to his past there, it might tip him over into drinking again. I imagine he's been hanging by a thread as it is. This is definitely not the moment for me to betray the friendship.'

'Don't be ridiculous. You're not betraying the friendship. Anyway, I need you here with me tonight more than he needs you over there. Surely it can wait till the morning? It's after eleven.'

'It's a big deal for Lang. I haven't seen him for a couple of months.'

Hennie let out her waking scream.

'There's a lot at stake for him.'

'Go then!' She picked up Hennie and stood. 'Just go!' She had to shout to make herself heard over Hennie's lusty screams.

Lang's front door was open, the porch light shining out across the downtrodden grass.

Andy parked at the kerb and got out of the car and locked it. The street was empty, the stillness of the London planes against the night sky, the only sign of life the lone figure of a woman in the distance walking a pair of small dogs. Andy stepped over the low brick wall and walked across to the front porch.

Lang came towards him along the passage. 'Thank you for coming, Andy.' There was an anxious formality about Lang's manner. He stepped to one side and Andy went in. Lang checked the garden then closed the front door.

They stood looking at each other. Each waiting for the other to speak first. Andy thought Lang looked caved in and ten years older.

'So, what's going on?' he asked.

'I'll tell you! I'll tell you!'

Lang hurried ahead. Andy followed him across the wide hall, their reflections approaching eerily in the antique mirror on the far wall. The air was still heavy with the stale smell of cigarettes.

In the kitchen there was no sign of the wine cask. The table with its scatter of catalogues and remnants of meals was just as messy as usual, but instead of a wine cask there were two mugs with tea bags in them. The kettle was on the gas, sending a homely spout of steam into the air. A blanket in the corner beside the door next to the rifle was obviously where the cat had been sleeping. There was no sign of her. Her food bowl had a scatter of brown pellets in it. 'Is the mother cat still with you?' Andy said.

'She's hiding. If you stay long enough, she will come out and have a look at you. Sit down!' He gestured at a chair. He was nervous and impatient. He sat down opposite Andy. His hand shook when he lit a cigarette. He placed his hand on a blue folder lying on the table in front of him and looked squarely at Andy but didn't speak for a while. Then he leaned forward and, in a voice not much above a whisper, as if he were afraid someone might overhear him, he said, 'I have a chance to buy a Sickert nude.' He sat back, watching to see the effect of his news on Andy. 'It has happened at last. It is to be my reward. How long have I waited? I have survived for this.'

Andy said, 'That's great.'

Lang smiled. 'Would you like a cup of tea?'

'Thanks.'

Lang got up and took the kettle off the gas. He came over to the table and poured boiling water onto the tea bags then put the kettle back on the gas before turning the gas off. He sat down and blew on his tea then took a careful sip. He sat gazing at Andy over the top of his steaming mug, which he was holding close to his mouth with both hands, wearing an inward, knowing smile.

'You think all such beliefs as fate and destiny are superstition. It's what the English think. The English are not superstitious. For the English the old gods died too long ago. The wonderful irony is, of course, that the English fear superstition too greatly to ever permit themselves to openly acknowledge its influence on their decisions. Which is why they deny it so angrily.' He laughed. It was a sudden small gust of amusement. Almost a hiccup.

Andy said, 'I'm not really English.' But perhaps Lang was including Australians in his idea of who was English. Lumping all white Australians into one.

'You're English enough, Andy. Believe me.'

Andy thought, *And you're Chinese enough*, but held back from saying it.

'We are what we are, Andy. And you are English.'

Andy preferred the drink-sodden, emotional Lang to this one. Lang had never behaved so insensitively with him before. It was a side of the man he hadn't witnessed. He had driven all the way out to Camberwell in the middle of the night as a favour to Lang, leaving Jo at home feeling upset and abandoned, only to have Lang insist that he was English!

'Simon Marot called me last night. You don't know Simon. He is Melbourne's leading international art dealer.'

Andy was wondering if Lang was really worth it. He was feeling ungenerous towards him and was determined not to be a pushover when Lang finally got around to asking for the favour he had in mind.

'Simon is also a scholar and has published several monographs of artists. He is unusual among dealers here. He is honest. A man of principle. A decent, modest man of considerable achievement. And he is still young. I knew his father, who was also a dealer. He passed on the business and its values to his son. But like all the others, there are times when Simon needs reassurance about an Australian painting, especially when there is no signature and the provenance is uncertain. Simon called this afternoon and asked me to come in and look at a Blackman for him. When we'd looked at the picture, which I told him was a very good fake, he thanked me and we left it at that. I have never made a mistake in my attributions of Australian paintings. It is my one real accomplishment. And Simon knows I never deal and that my opinions can be trusted to be free of self-interest. We were in the back room of his High Street gallery. He turned the Blackman to the wall after I told him it was a fake. Blackman is easy to fake for anyone ruthless enough and skilled enough to do it, someone trained in the craft of painting. And there are many of them out there. I have met quite a few who make an indecent living at it.'

Lang paused and took a drink of tea. He lit a cigarette and coughed.

Andy was wondering how he would describe this moment later.

'Simon and I had been standing there talking about one thing and another for a few minutes, and I was thinking it was time for me to leave, when he said he had something to show me. As I said, Simon is straight, he's not into sneaky deals, so I was surprised to note that his manner had changed and he showed signs of being nervous. Perhaps nervous is not exactly the word. A kind of ambivalence came into his manner. It was as if, while we'd been chatting about trivial things, he had been considering whether or not to tell me about this other thing, and now he had suddenly decided to go ahead and tell me, but doing so had required him to go against his better judgement. I may be an alcoholic, but I'm not a fool. I am observant of people and I saw this uncertainty in Simon and I was intrigued. It was nothing too obvious but enough to alert me.'

Andy was looking at the blue folder on the table. Lang was keeping his free hand on it while he spoke.

'Simon said, *Come and have a look. I think it will interest you.* And I saw that, in saying this, he was fully committed, his nervous uncertainty pushed to one side. His father's moral code, if it was that, thrust to one side. Naturally, I was wary now. He led me over to the desk he sometimes uses in the back room and he reached down and lifted out from behind it a framed oil that made me gasp. I literally took a step back. He laid the painting face up on the desk and was watching for my reaction. My agitation must have been obvious to him. I was no longer alert but was taken completely off my guard. The painting he had laid on the desk was a Sickert nude painted *contre-jour*. It was *the* painting I have dreamed of owning since I first discovered the works of Sickert while I was still a young student at art school, in the days even before Agatha and I were married. Seeing the Sickert nude lying on Simon's desk, right there within my reach, the days of my innocence flared into my mind with a vividness that overwhelmed me. It was quite as if a clock struck the hour and everything I had come to doubt was to be restored to me, the mystery made at once clear and open. My hour had come. That is what I felt. An emotion I have never felt before. A clock striking is a poor metaphor for what I experienced when I saw the Sickert lying there on Simon's desk. What I experienced was the power of fate.'

'Fate,' Andy said, smiling. 'Was it?' His resentment was gone. He was enjoying Lang's enthusiasm.

'When I tell you in a minute what happened earlier in the day you will understand. Simon's production of the Sickert was the second of two things that came magically into alignment. Simon told me he had been asked by a prominent Melbourne family to act for them in the private sale of the painting. So, the nude was available! It was not just lying there for me to admire. It was for sale. I could hold it in my hands if I wished to. Simon invited me to pick it up and examine it. My hands shook as I lifted it from the desk and held it before my face. *Mine! You have always been mine!* My tears of joy remained within me, but they were real. I wept for myself, for Agatha, for my youth and for my lost dreams. I stood looking at the Sickert nude and I wept for art, for my love and my hopes, and for my failure. Nothing has ever before meant so much to me.

Simon knows of my obsession with owning a Sickert nude. I asked him if the family were in a hurry to make the sale and he said that they were.'

He fell silent and sat back and lit a fresh cigarette, his hand trembling.

Andy said, 'Amazing! I suppose you'll sell some of your collection, will you?'

'Oh no! No. That can't be done. To sell a painting takes time. It must be illustrated in an important sale catalogue and become a thing jealously coveted by the people whose collections will be augmented by its inclusion. To get your price you need a strong underbidder. A passionate underbidder, if you can find one.'

'That's not what your dealer is doing with this Sickert? How much are they asking for it?'

'This picture is an exception. The owners asked Marot to sell it privately. They don't want it to be seen in a public auction. They don't want the family to be talked about.'

Andy was thinking that surely Lang would kill for a glass of wine at this moment,

'I said I will buy it. Thirty-five thousand. I don't have that kind of money sitting around. I didn't care. My eyes did not leave the painting even for a moment. *Can you give me a couple of weeks to raise the cash?* I asked. He did not seem at all surprised by my offer. He would have to check with the owners but he was sure they would agree. She is standing at the window with her back to the viewer, gazing out into the day, the light shimmering around the outlines of her body, giving life and movement to her flesh.'

He paused and Andy watched him drag deeply on his cigarette, as if he hoped to get from the shot of nicotine the kind of helpless joy alcohol had given him in the past.

'One more thing that made my astonishment justified. This is the very painting that must have matured from an idea expressed in this pencil sketch which I bought more than twenty years ago.' He opened the blue folder that lay on the table under his hand and took a sketch from it. He turned the drawing so that Andy could examine it.

It was a pencil drawing of a naked woman at a window with her back to the viewer. The paper on which the drawing had been made was squared up in preparation for a larger, more finished version. Lang said, 'You can see here the magic with which Sickert imbued these few simple pencil lines. We must marvel at how the grace of the idea is realised by the hand of the artist.' He laughed softly. 'How amazing is it? I'm standing there in Simon Marot's back room looking at the painting born from the very sketched idea that's been in my possession for more than twenty years. When I say it's the picture I've been dreaming of all this time, this is what I mean. As I stood there, holding the fully realised oil painting in my hands, I experienced a powerful hallucination. The conviction that I was holding before my face a picture that I had painted myself, but in some other time, even in some other life almost. And for a moment, while the power of the hallucination persisted, I was no longer the failed artist Lang Tzu, but became Sickert. Or he became me. It was the same thing. This strange and wonderful feeling engulfed me in a state of perfect happiness, and for that moment my defeat was wiped from my life. I had succeeded after all. I had achieved what I had set out to achieve when I was an idealistic young man. My failure and defeat, not this moment, had been the illusion. This, at last, was the real. I had broken through. I had embraced art and art had accepted my embrace.'

Clearly agitated, Lang stood up and stepped across to the window over the sink. 'I thought she might have come out to take a look at you by now.' He stood for some time looking out into the dark garden, the bare branches of the old pear tree out there catching the light from the window. He turned to Andy at last and said, 'Not everything may be lost.' He waited, observing Andy's reaction closely. 'If you help me get this Sickert, I will owe you more than friendship.'

'Bullshit!' Andy said. 'You don't owe me anything now and you never will owe me anything. But how can I possibly help? Jo and I don't have any money.'

'It's not money I need from you,' Lang said. He dragged on his cigarette, his eyes narrowed against the smoke. 'It's complicated.' He frowned. 'It's complicated,' he repeated. 'You're the only one who can do it.' His manner had sobered, the high energy of the episode was spent.

Andy noticed that the skin of Lang's cheeks and his forehead was glossy and his chin entirely free of any hint of a beard. Despite his hollowed-out look of having been aged by his recent experiences, Lang had scarcely a wrinkle on his face. His hair was cut short. It was thick and coarse and stood up from his scalp like a crew cut, spiky and black, without any grey. He came back and sat down in his chair again. 'I went to Sullivans' viewing this morning. The first of the two things that came into alignment today happened at Sullivans this morning. In the back room, where you bought the naive painting with the Chinese man in it, I saw a large, torn and very grimy canvas stuffed into a soap carton with other rubbish. If I were to show an interest in it tomorrow, the dealers' scouts would pounce and bid me up to my limit.' He looked at Andy. 'This is our moment, Andy.'

'So you want me to go into Sullivans in the morning and bid on this Chinese treasure for you?'

'It's not a Chinese treasure. It's a landscape painting. It's been missing for years. I first saw it when I was at art school. It was owned in those days by one of the school's instructors. He didn't know what to do with it. It was a problem. It's still a problem. He used to invite a small group of us to his place for drinks. He kept the picture in his spare room with its face to the wall. Most people didn't know he had it. Unsigned and atypical of the style and the artist's subjects. But it's him all right.'

'Who are we talking about?'

'Sir Arthur Streeton.'

'I'm not exactly an expert, Lang, but even I would know an Arthur Streeton if I saw one.'

'Not this one you wouldn't. It is generally believed that, despite Streeton's rural landscapes, he never painted farm animals. He disdained the cloying romanticism in the way farm animals were depicted by his contemporaries and didn't want to be identified with them. Streeton saw himself as being above that kind of thing. His was a superior attitude. He believed he was an artist with a higher calling that distinguished him from his contemporaries. This picture was too difficult for the instructor to handle. He would have sold it but he didn't know how to. He never worked out what to do with it. After he died, I lost sight of it. It's had a hard life since then. Someone's put a hole through it and the stretcher's broken. The subject's not typical of Streeton, but it's him. I'd say it's probably a composition he regretted doing but he never got around to overpainting it for a reason we'll never know.' He drew on his smoke, visualising the painting. 'It has a lot of problems besides its subject. No signature, no provenance and it's not typical.' He waited a moment. 'And, of course, it's in a terrible condition. It will have to be brought back from the dead.'

Andy said nothing.

Lang was studying him. 'You will have to sell it to Bartos for me.'

Andy laughed. 'Me? You must be kidding.'

Lang gave a small lift of his shoulders. 'It won't work if Bartos knows I'm involved.'

'You're serious? I don't know the first thing about selling art. You've always said selling it is as much of an art as making it.'

'I will tell you what you must do. No dealer will buy it from you for the kind of money you can ask from Bartos. Bartos looks the part of a gentleman of the arts. He promotes himself in the market as the expert on Australian art. But he's not. He's a salesman. Bartos is an expert at selling. They are always the easiest people to sell to. He doesn't know the first thing about Australian or any other art. He has advisers. Without his advisers he's in the dark. The name Streeton and an important gilt corner frame will have him salivating. He will be suspicious, but he won't want to risk losing something special. He'll want to call his adviser. And he'll want to know where you got it from. You tell him an old Melbourne family want to sell the picture for cash with no fuss. He'll understand that.'

'Hang on! Hang on, Lang. I haven't said I'll do it yet. It sounds as if this Bartos bloke would see the problem at once.'

Lang looked at him resolutely. 'There is no one else I can ask to do this for me. You are my only friend.'

18

It was early Wednesday morning and Jo was sitting at the bench in the kitchen feeding Hennie with a plastic spoon. She was still wearing her dressing-gown, her own bowl of muesli and tinned pears on the bench in front of her, a tub of yoghurt next to the bowl. It was raining again. A steady cold rain that had set in during the night, the air still holding the chill of the ocean it had crossed to reach them, that great empty stretch of sea out there to the south-west of the port.

Andy was at the stove waiting for the coffee, his toast and a jar of marmalade on one of Jo's favourite blue plates on the bench closer to the back door. He had a headache and was tired from his late night. After getting home he had sat in his workroom and written up his notes of the evening with Lang. He loved the private world of his notes and it was three in the morning before he stopped writing and went upstairs and climbed into bed beside Jo, his mind still awash with thoughts and ideas, his gut feeling against Lang's request unresolved.

Jo said, 'If you're so worried about it, give him a ring and tell him you can't do it.'

Andy poured the steaming coffee into his mug. 'There's no one else he can ask. If he doesn't get this Sickert nude it may be the end of him.' What Andy was thinking but not saying was that if he didn't buy the broken Streeton for Lang, it might mean the end of their friendship, and the end of the unfolding story in his notebooks.

Jo dreaded being late for work. Punctuality was important to her. They relied on her at the bookshop. She was valued and trusted and she loved the job. Andy was sitting at the end of the bench eating his toast and watching her. She said, 'Can you take her, darling? I'm going to be late if I don't get in the shower right now.' Andy went over and wiped the food off Hennie's cheeks and took her out of her highchair and set her on the floor with the yellow plastic tipper truck that she loved. She pushed the truck ahead of her out into the dining room.

Jo stood at the bench spooning up her muesli, swallowing it without chewing. She spoke with her mouth full. 'It's totally unrealistic of Lang to imagine that owning this Sickert will solve his problems. And anyway, I just can't see you selling this dud picture for him. It's not you. You'll hate yourself for it.'

Leaving her half-eaten bowl of muesli on the bench, she went through into the bathroom. She called back, 'I love you!'

After dropping Hennie off at the creche, Andy drove over to Richmond. Jo sometimes reminded him of his father, the way she stuck to her values no matter what. He parked the car and walked across the road to Sullivans auction house. A broken deal table lay on its side by the front door, to its left on the footpath an elaborate Victorian credenza with a door missing and no mirror.

Inside, the front room was crammed with old furniture from deceased estates. The auctioneer was selling a set of twelve balloon-backed dining chairs with a damaged carver. Someone had lived the dream of grand dinners with guests seated around their table. A dead person now. The smell of the auction room was of something old and dusty and filled with a kind of hopeless decay, the feeling that people had given up and abandoned life, the clearance of deceased estates, the rubbish no one wanted, except these dubious-looking men hanging around hoping for a bargain, scavengers roaming about the place among the leftovers of lives once lived, going around touching this and that, lifting lids and opening drawers and bending down to look under things, giving each other sidelong looks. Men for the most part, sniffing around, pretending to be indifferent to the auctioneer.

Andy felt as if he were in danger of being mistaken for one of them. Standing there by the front entrance he saw that Sullivans was the home of failure. This was where they gathered, all these old men who had accomplished nothing fine or decent during their lives. When he was here to buy the naive painting for Lang, the atmosphere of Sullivans hadn't bothered him. He had felt himself to be in no danger then of becoming a regular in this place of squalor and failure, with its sour smell of the dead past. Lang had suggested that, with his guidance, Andy might be able to give up teaching and make enough from dealing to give himself over full-time to his writing. He didn't like teaching, but he seriously loathed the thought of ever becoming a dealer. It would be sliding into despair.

He followed the auctioneer, joining the press of scavengers as they headed into the back room. He saw the damaged painting at once, just as Lang had described it. It had been thrust carelessly into a tall cardboard carton, the snapped stretcher rising up like the broken leg of a wooden crutch. He couldn't see the painted image but saw only the reverse of the old canvas, where it had been violently folded back hard against itself so that it could be squeezed into the box.

Andy was suddenly nervous. The auctioneer handed a page from his clipboard to his assistant and called out the first lot number on the new page. Andy's hand flew up and he called out, 'Ten dollars!' Men turned to look at him. The questions in their yellowed eyes: *Why the eagerness? Who's he? What's he got hold of? How come we missed that?*

Ten minutes later the auction was done and the auctioneer had headed off to the pub across the road for a counter lunch and a beer. Andy waited in line at the window to the office. He presented his chit to the woman and paid ten dollars then went to the back room and collected the box. At the car he drew the painting out of the box and laid it on the back seat, still folded onto itself, the image of the head of a Clydesdale folded in half, a glimpse of a dusty summer road and hills, blued and paled by distance. The broken stretcher as awkward as a bone projecting from the leg of an accident victim. The whole enterprise disgusted him. He abandoned the carton and its collection of doorknobs and rusty hinges on the footpath and drove over to Lang's.

Lang met him at the front door. He took the picture from Andy, nervous and eager, saying nothing. Andy followed him through to the kitchen. Lang had cleared off the table. He unfolded the canvas and laid it flat on the table with the painted side down. Andy stood by his shoulder. The smell of the auction room floated up from the painting, something dead. There was a long rip through the middle of the canvas and a hole the size of a dinner plate towards the top. Lang studied the marks on the back of the canvas, leaning over it and touching it here and there, rubbing away some of the filth with the side of his hand. He said nothing. Then, after a few minutes, he turned the canvas over. The plate-sized hole was where a range of hills stood far off in the distance. Lang fitted the edges of the tear together and stepped back. He lit a cigarette and stood looking at the painting. A grand Australian landscape it might once have been. Two massive shire horses were hauling a cart loaded with timber up a cutting on the side of a hill overlooking a valley in the middle distance. A man, the carter, walking beside the near-side horse. He was carrying a long whip and smoking a pipe. The two beasts were straining, leaning into the load, heads down, the muscles of their powerful shoulders tensed. The picture must have been exposed to smoke at some time during its life. It was darkened and stained where something had been spilled on it. There was no evidence of a signature.

Andy said, 'So if Streeton really did paint this, why didn't he sign it? You said he always signed his pictures. This is an ambitious painting. It's not something he could have done quickly then forgotten about.'

'Our problem,' Lang said, 'is that there is only one man we can sell it to. If we fail to sell it to Bartos at our first attempt, we'll be stuck with it. A chequered history such as this work has offers us no second chance. The art market is ruthless. Bartos is one of only two dealers in this city whose reputation depends on the buyers' trust in his claim to be the leading expert in Australian art. He knows he's vulnerable, so he'll be suspicious. He can be a scary person to deal with. If you get on the wrong side of Bartos he can be very unpleasant. He has people who will do his bidding, if you know what I mean. He thinks we're all as nasty as he is himself.' Lang turned his head and considered Andy for a long moment. 'It could be unpleasant for you.'

Andy said nothing.

'You're not troubled by this?'

'Of course I'm troubled,' Andy said. 'I may yet decide not to go through with it.'

'I don't want you to get involved in something you don't understand.'

'Are *you* troubled?'

'For myself, no. Bartos can't touch me. But you're an outsider. I can't protect you. The other specialist Australian dealer is Maggie Sewell, but we can't offer it to her. Maggie's the real thing. She would know of this painting's existence, if only by rumour, and she wouldn't touch it. Not because it isn't by Streeton; it is by Streeton. She wouldn't touch it because it's a problem. It's not only probably unfinished but was most likely abandoned by Streeton. If you were to study his catalogue raisonné you wouldn't find it described there. There is no record, either published or on the back of the canvas, of its having ever been shown in an exhibition. So it's not just the lack of a signature that's a problem. It's not that simple. And that can be overcome if there is sound provenance. Worst of all, probably, is its subject: carthorses. Farm animals are a subject Streeton specialists know the artist claimed never to paint. He despised the work of those artists who painted endless romantic scenes of cattle in the early rays of the sun's light or majestic carthorses like these two. Our Streeton is the kind of picture that would be challenged if it were ever to appear in a serious auction catalogue. It is trouble. And Maggie doesn't want trouble. Margaret Sewell knows very well that Streeton claimed he didn't paint horses. So, if it's genuine, why is this picture dominated by two shire horses? And it will have been extensively cleaned and recently restored when she sees it. Maja's work is very fine, it's the finest there is in this town—she trained in Budapest and Paris with the best of them—but Maggie would detect her restorations.'

Andy noticed how calm Lang was. He even seemed to be enjoying himself.

'Maggie Sewell's knowledge is encyclopaedic. She knows almost as much about Australian art as I do. More, possibly. Her connections span generations. She's been watching the merry-go-round of art sales in this town forever. She must be in her eighties by now.'

He looked at Andy and grinned, a mischievous grin that made him look slightly mad. 'But all the same, Maggie will be important to us in this sale. Within a day of us making our sale, she will know everything about it. But she will never admit she knows. She doesn't acknowledge the existence of Bartos. For Maggie Sewell, Bartos may as well be dealing in fish at the market. He is too far beneath her to be visible in her world. He gives the profession a bad name. Bartos is a bootmaker from Hungary who happens to sell pictures in Melbourne. Without his advisers, Bartos is lost. The massive gilt frame and the name Sir Arthur Streeton will dazzle him. He'll be suspicious. But he'll be afraid to turn it down. Suppose it's the real thing and he misses it? First off, he'll ask you if you'd mind him calling one of his advisers.'

'And what will I say to that?'

'You'll say of course not. Go ahead.'

'You're looking forward to it,' Andy said. 'Why can't you do this yourself? You know these people. They know you. It's your world, not mine.'

'They know I'd never sell a picture such as this unless there was something wrong with it. And if there was nothing wrong with it, and for some reason I did want to sell it—for the money, say—why wouldn't I put it into one of the respectable auctions where they would have to compete for it? They'd laugh at me if I offered it to them. They'd think I'd developed Alzheimer's. But you are completely unknown to them. A fresh face in off the street. A clear-eyed innocent. And you're acting for a friend, aren't you? You don't know anything about this painting or the art world. You don't need to know anything. Your friend, whose family has owned the painting forever, wants to sell it without going public, for her own private reasons. Maybe she's doing her brother and sister out of some of the inheritance. Settling an old score. Something like that. Who knows? Make it up. You're the storyteller. You don't know and you don't need to know. Plead ignorance. Leave Bartos wondering. You tell him, first off, if he's not interested, your client has told you to offer it to Margaret Sewell. That's all you know. That'll make him take you seriously. There is no one he hates more or envies more than Margaret Sewell. Don't forget to mention her name within five seconds of entering his gallery.'

'And what if he asks why I've taken it to him first?'

'You've been advised by your friend that he, Bartos, is the leading expert in Australian art sales, not Margaret Sewell. He's the numero uno. Flatter him. He's the man who knows everything. You are the man who knows nothing. According to your friend, Sewell's the number two, *he's* the man to see. Your friend said he would know. He'll like that. It puts him ahead of Maggie for once in his life. He's never had that before.'

'How much do I have to ask him to give me for the picture?'

'Let's say twenty-five thousand. As much of it in cash as he has in his safe.'

'Are you serious?'

'First we have to have it restored and cleaned. I'll call Maja and get her to come over and pick it up. I'll tell her it's urgent. The family who own the Sickert aren't going to wait forever.' He lit a fresh cigarette and looked at Andy.

'So how's the no drinking going?' Andy said, and wished at once he hadn't said it. But he was feeling resentful of Lang and not looking forward to having to deal with this Bartos character.

Lang smiled. Or maybe it was a grimace. 'I have been forbidden to ever see my first love again, for the rest of my life.' He studied Andy for a few long seconds. 'I have been exiled once again. Forgive me, but it's not easy.'

'I'm sorry. I shouldn't have asked.'

Lang said nothing.

Andy realised it was time for him to leave. 'I'd better go. I have to pick up Hennie in an hour.'

At the front door, Lang said, 'I'll call you when Maja has finished with it.'

Andy knew he was being told not to visit Lang again until he heard from him. Being together without the wine must be a terrible strain for Lang. He didn't seem to know how to be himself without the wine to liberate his spirit. He was just holding on, acting a part, being an idea of himself, an idea he loathed.

Andy stepped over the wall and turned and gave Lang a farewell wave. Lang stood at his door. He didn't return Andy's wave. Andy wondered for the first time if he was going to make it.

19

Andy drove to the creche and picked up Hennie. She had a snotty nose. Her puffy little cheeks were red and she was in a grumpy mood. He gave her a cuddle before strapping her into her car seat. At home he changed her on the dining room table. He worked the safety pin through the thick wad of the nappy and picked her up, holding her against his chest and rocking her, his right hand rubbing her back. He sang softly the words of 'When the Yeller's on the Broom', an old Scottish song from the summer walkers that his father had sung. He was looking across the dining table, a cheap trestle they'd covered with an Afghan rug. Hanging on the wall opposite him was the only piece of art he and Jo possessed. It was a watercolour of a flat landscape around Romney Marsh, painted by his father when his father and mother went for a holiday there when they were both old. When his father died, Andy went to England to see his mother. He stayed with her for two weeks. One evening, she took the watercolour from the deep drawer in the bottom of the china cabinet where his father had kept his unframed drawings and watercolours and gave it to Andy. 'Your father wanted you to have this.'

He stood here now comforting Hennie and looking across the room at the painting of the flat open country with the glistening waterway meandering through fields covered in the yellow flowers of what he took to be a crop of rape. He could smell his father's pipe tobacco, the memory of his father's words in his mind: *We learn our way by searching for it.* It was a simple enough philosophy, but Andy had never been sure if he was following it or not. With the notebooks, however, wasn't he finding his own way at last? Hadn't he begun to see that he had in the steady accumulation of his notes the subject and the style of what must surely become his first book? Was it to be a novel or some kind of memoir? He didn't know. It didn't matter. He didn't care if it was neither. It was writing, it gave him great pleasure, and he would persist with it, of that much he was certain, so long as he and Lang persisted. It had become precious to him. He entered the private world of the notebooks confidently. Re-reading his writing, he heard the conviction of it.

When Jo got home and took Hennie off his hands, he would go into his workroom and write up his notes of today's meeting with Lang. He pushed aside the thought he'd had earlier that Lang might not be going to survive. Would he include that troubling impression in the notes? He carried Hennie upstairs and walked her back and forth until she fell asleep, then he laid her carefully in her cot and covered her with her blue teddy blanket. He sat awhile to make sure she was asleep then went back downstairs, leaving all the doors open in case she woke up. Jo would be home soon.

Jo was late. Hennie had woken a while ago from her afternoon nap. She was hot and unhappy. He sat at the bench in the kitchen with her on his knees and tried feeding her banana puree. She grimaced when the spoon touched her lips, and if a little of the puree did make its way into her mouth, she pushed it out again with her tongue, a look of disgust on her face. He set the spoon aside and stood up and walked her up and down the kitchen, singing to her, the sound of his voice lost against her wailing. The Greeks next door would surely think she was being tormented. Every few minutes she ran out of steam and stopped yelling, taking deep, sobbing gulps of air, her nose running with yellow snot, which he wiped away with his handkerchief, her face wet, her cheeks bright red. The thermometer was upstairs in her room. He carried her up and took her temperature. She screamed when it touched her ear. She had a slight temperature, hovering around thirty-eight. Where was Jo? Whenever she was late like this, he worried that something terrible had happened to her. The worst tram disaster in forty years. He could see the headline. He carried Hennie downstairs and out into the kitchen again. He was wondering what to do next when he heard the front door slam. 'Thank God! Here's your mother.' Hennie fell silent.

Jo came into the kitchen. She looked radiantly beautiful, her light green silk scarf at her throat, her short dark hair mussed by the wind, her lovely two-tone grey Italian coat unbuttoned, her Irish tweed skirt and her ribbed stockings. He said, 'You look bloody fantastic!'

'I've got some exciting news. Armand insists I visit the owners of the letters. They still live on the property and want to meet me. They'll give the project a contemporary context.' She looked at Hennie and frowned. 'Is she okay? I'm sorry I'm late, but Armand can be very insistent. Now you're going to be late.'

'I'll call in sick. I think she's got a bit of a temperature.'

'I'll take her as soon as I've changed and had a wash.'

Hennie was reaching for her mother and screaming again, snot running freely from her nose, her nostrils red and sore.

Jo said, 'The poor little darling. Have you been using the new cream? I won't be a minute.' She went out to get changed.

Andy stood at the back door looking into the narrow plot of garden between the two side fences, holding the exhausted child to his chest and rocking back and forth. He said aloud, 'Normal family life, little one. Get used to it.' He wanted to be making love to Jo. She had looked so wonderfully exotic and self-confident when she came home. At thirty she was maturing into her beauty, becoming more herself. Would she want to have another child? Not long after they met she said that to have an only child was selfish and was not really creating a family. How would they manage with two screamers like this one?

That night, after Hennie finally went off to sleep, Andy and Jo made love. It wasn't the first time since Hennie's arrival eighteen months earlier, but it was the first time since they had become parents that the old intensity of their early lust for each other had swept through them. Folded in Andy's arms afterwards, Jo went off to sleep at once. She woke half an hour later and murmured, 'Are you awake?' They made love again and laughed at themselves, then lay there telling each other about the events of their day. She was excited about the project of the letters. He began to tell her about the importance of the notebooks for him. He suddenly needed her to understand why he was helping Lang with the deal. He wanted her to understand, and to share some of his enthusiasm. 'I'm writing something at last that feels important to me,' he said.

'Yes, I know. I've been wondering when you'd tell me about it.'

Even now Andy was aware of them both half listening out for Hennie, talking in low voices. He said, 'Hennie has made the three of us become each other in a way I could not have imagined before she came along.'

20

It was still warm and sunny when Jo and Andy came home from the local park with Hennie. There was a message from Lang. Jo stopped in the passage with the stroller, Hennie fast asleep after exhausting herself playing with another toddler on the small slide. Jo waited while Andy played the message. *'Maja just dropped it off. Come and have a look.'* It was the first Andy had heard from Lang for three weeks.

He and Jo looked at each other. Jo said, 'Are you going to do it?'

'I think you know I am.'

'You can still decide not to. He never deals, he says, so you're being asked to do the deal for him. Is that fair? He's not stupid. I don't believe for a minute it will end your friendship with him if you explain why you don't want to do it. Just tell him it's not straightforward for you.' When he didn't say anything to this, she said, 'Maybe you secretly *want* to do it. Is that it?' She laughed. 'Has this become a bit of a man thing for you? You're not being honest, not with yourself or me or with Lang. Is your friendship with him worth writing about if you lose it because you won't do this?'

'You're making it sound more complicated than it is. If I don't sell the Streeton for him he'll have no hope of raising the cash to make an offer on the Sickert. It's as simple as that.'

'No it isn't. You know it's not that simple, not for us. And so what if he doesn't get the Sickert? You know the painting's not going to solve Lang's problems. You'd be more of a friend to him if you had the courage to tell him you can't do it.'

They stood, not speaking, Andy looking down at Hennie lying there in her innocent sleep. Jo said, 'You're not looking at me because you know I hate the idea of you doing this. It's just not you. It's not *us*. It's not the man I fell in love with on the bus to Sydney. I knew you when I first saw you that day. I felt dizzy when you smiled back and sat down next to me. The man I met that day wouldn't do this. And what would your father think? Have you thought of that?'

He looked at her. 'Of course I've thought of it. But it's not a crime. You make it sound as if I'd be breaking the law. It's just the way the art market works.'

'That's bullshit!' She was looking at Hennie now. She said gloomily, 'I'm afraid of it. It's going to cost us something. It's not *us*. It might not be criminal, but it's not honest all the same.' She looked at Andy. 'It's a crooked deal and you know that, and you're conflicted about it because you know it's dishonourable, and even if you succeed in doing it you'll never be proud of having done it. It's sneaky. The man I met on the bus wouldn't do it. What would Hennie think if she knew her father would do this kind of thing?'

'You're overdoing it.'

'No I'm not. I'm being honest. I just hate the whole fucking idea! It's not fair of Lang to ask you to do it. He's using you. It's not your world; it's his. You don't understand it. If you don't do it, he'll ask someone else to do it for him. What about that shady friend of his who was going to shoot the mother cat? I bet he'd do it without turning a hair.'

He leaned forward and kissed her on the lips. 'I love you!'

'I love you too.'

'Take her up. I'll bring the tea.'

'Are you going to ring him back?'

He didn't answer.

'Ring him now, for my sake, and at least tell him you want to talk to him about it before committing yourself. It's not just you; it's me and Hennie too. I don't want to have to think of you doing this deal. You'll be betraying your father's values. You know you will. This is not what art has always meant to you. What your father gave you is precious. Not everyone gets that in this life. A strong parent who knows what their values are and sticks to them. It's precious. When we first met, you used to say art was your consolation. I loved that about you. Will you still be confident of that?'

He said, 'You're idealising my father. He was a man, just like any other.'

'He was your hero! You'll destroy that. You'll regret it. And what about this other dealer, the real expert? What's her name?'

'Margaret Sewell.'

'From what you said, she's soon going to know about this painting being sold to Bartos. Is she going to keep that information to herself? People don't keep these things to themselves. She and Bartos are enemies, you said. She'll spread it around that Bartos bought a dud.'

'It's not a dud.'

'It's suspect. You can't stop these things from becoming known.'

Hennie made a choking sound and woke with a start. She began to cry.

Jo leaned down and ran her fingers softly over Hennie's scalp. 'I'd better go and change her and give her a feed.' She looked up at Andy. 'Bring me up a cup of tea and one of those Anzacs, will you please?'

Jo unstrapped Hennie and carried her up the stairs. She called back, 'Ring him now!'

Andy folded up the stroller and stowed it in the cupboard under the stairs. He could hear Hennie crying upstairs. She abruptly fell silent. He went out to the kitchen and put the jug on to boil. He poured the boiling water into the teapot and sluiced it around, warming the pot before putting in the tea-leaves. Jo refused to use tea bags. She loved the ritual of the plain old brown teapot she'd been given years ago by Aunt Henrietta. He loved it too. Standing waiting for the tea to draw, he said aloud, 'Loyalty to friendship counts for something too, doesn't it?'

The Streeton was leaning against the table with the vase of dead hydrangeas on it in the front sitting room. The portrait of Agatha gazing over her shoulder at the scene from above the fireplace, that look of regretful farewell in her beautiful dark eyes. The Streeton was in an elaborate gilt frame. The framing gave to the painting the convincing appearance of an important Australian Heidelberg School landscape by the great man himself, Sir Arthur, the archenemy of Australian modernism. Except, of course, there was no signature.

Lang came over and stood beside Andy. Together they studied the painting of the two powerful Clydesdales toiling up the hill, the harness taut, their load of timber looming behind them. Andy thought, *Beasts of burden*. The restorer had removed the layers of smoke and grime and revealed a bright expanse of graded tones, an Australian summer day, the landscape shimmering into the blue distance of heat and stillness. Andy could almost hear the magpies. He squatted and searched the surface closely but could see no sign of where the rip in the canvas or the plate-sized hole had been repaired. He stood up slowly and stepped back.

Lang said, 'What do you think?'

'It's amazing.'

'Maja's the best in the business.'

'And expensive too, I bet?'

Lang said, 'Call Bartos around eleven in the morning. He'll be in his gallery by then, and probably alone. I'll get a blanket for it. It's going to fit in your station wagon.' Lang was all business and eager to get on with it.

'Jo doesn't feel good about me doing this.'

'Wives are always going to question whatever we do.'

Andy laughed and looked at him. 'Jo's not *wives*. She's got a point.'

'I didn't mean that the way it sounded.' Lang lit a cigarette and stood smoking, his eyes screwed up, looking at the painting. He said thoughtfully, 'It really is Australian, isn't it?'

'It's not that.'

'At his best he was brilliant, and interesting; his small Art Nouveau pieces are exquisite. But this isn't something I'd ever want in my collection.' He was deep in thought. 'He didn't like it himself. So why didn't he scrape it back and reuse the canvas for something else? Canvas was expensive.'

When Lang didn't say any more, Andy asked, 'So why didn't he?'

'I don't know. Maybe the whole exercise depressed him. Maybe he regretted painting these horses. Maybe he felt as if he'd betrayed his values and joined the artists whose work he most despised. Not the modernists, but his own mob. The lesser ones. But he couldn't help feeling a bit proud of these horses. They are magnificently there in front of us, aren't they?'

'We'll be dudding Bartos if he falls for it. That's what Jo hates. I don't like it either, but . . .'

Lang said nothing for a moment or two, then he said mildly, 'Don't do it if you think you're going to regret it.' There was just a small edge of something unsaid in his tone.

'I didn't say I wasn't going to do it.' He couldn't think of what it was that Jo had said. She had made her objections clear, and they had been persuasive, but what had she actually said?

They were both silent. Andy looked at Lang. 'I'll do it,' he said. 'It's for friendship.' He knew this was a lie. He was doing it for himself, for his writing.

Lang said softly, 'Thank you.'

On the way home Andy stopped off at South Melbourne Market and bought two chicken breast fillets and a bottle of riesling. He carried the heavy picture inside and left it in the hall, its face to the wall, the old pink blanket from Lang's place draped over it. He stood listening to the house. It was still and silent and very empty. Without Jo and Hennie, would he be doing this? He was doing it for Lang and for the continuation of the notebooks. The promise of the notebooks, the sheer solitary pleasure of writing them, that was for Jo and Hennie, for the three of them, for the success of the family. But more than anything, it was for himself. The freedom he had found in his writing. He loved it. Sitting alone in his workroom with the door closed, labouring in his own world. With those notes he knew himself to be an honest man. His father would have understood. He was sure of that.

He went through to the kitchen and put the fillets and the wine in the fridge. There was a note on the bench.

We've taken the tram in to meet Armand and Diana.
Don't worry about dinner, I'll shop on the way home.
I hope you went all right. All my love, your Jo xxx

He returned to the hall, picked up the picture and carried it through to the sitting room where they spent their evenings. He took the blanket off and stood looking at it, then he picked it up and set it on the mantelpiece above the fireplace and stepped back.

The front door slammed and he heard Jo's laughter and Hennie's happy voice. They came into the room.

Jo said, 'Oh my God, is that it? It's amazing. It completely changes the feel of this room. It's like having a window looking out onto the countryside. It's beautiful, darling. We should keep it.' She laughed and came over and kissed him. 'It's a pity there's none of Aunt Hennie's money left. We could buy it. How much did you say Lang wanted for it?'

'Twenty-five. We could buy ourselves a cottage in the country for that kind of money.'

'Or renovate this place properly.'

He said, 'I don't like it, anyway. I couldn't live with a thing like that looming over us.'

'Well, I think it's wonderful.' She turned Hennie to face it. 'What do you think, Bubble?'

Hennie pointed at the picture and said something in her special language.

Andy said, 'Bubble? Are we calling her Bubble now?'

'Diana called her Bubble. Armand gave her a beautiful old book of French fairytales for when she's grown up a bit. It's in my bag. I'll show you after she's had her bath.'

He took the painting down and covered it with Lang's blanket and carried it out into the hallway. His mood was sullen and heavy. When he came back into the sitting room, Jo had laid Hennie on the couch and was leaning over her and tickling her, Hennie laughing, her hands grabbing at the air. 'You *are* a little bubble, aren't you, darling?'

He stood looking at them, wishing he could lighten up and join in. The deal weighed on him now. He was no longer sure of what he would do.

21

After Jo had gone into work, he dropped Hennie off at the creche and went home and waited for eleven o'clock to come around. He was nervous, sitting at the bench in the kitchen nursing a second coffee. He was looking out the side window over the sink, seeing the open door of the washhouse and the old Rheem water heater that was rusting around the bottom and beginning to leak, a puddle of brown stuff gathered in the corner. It was another thing that was going to need replacing. He was repeating Margaret Sewell's name over in his head. He was worried that her name would leave his head the minute he needed it. He had written *Margaret Sewell* on a scrap of paper and put it in his shirt pocket. But what good would that do him? He couldn't very well pull it out and refer to it in front of Bartos. He was feeling the kind of fluttery anxiety he used to feel at the swimming pool when he was being made to dive from the middle board. It was fear. Why fear? What could Bartos do to him? That slightly insane look that passed across Lang's features when he said their deal with Bartos would be known to Margaret Sewell almost as soon as it happened. He looked at his watch again. The minute hand had scarcely moved.

At ten to eleven he went out to the hall and sat looking at the phone. On the dot of eleven he picked up the phone and called the number Lang had given him.

A young female voice said, 'Bartos Gallery.'

'I wish to speak to Mr Bartos. I have a painting I believe may interest him.'

'Mr Bartos is very busy. Can I give him a message?'

'I'd rather speak to him directly.'

'May I ask who I'm speaking to?'

'My name is Andy McPherson. He doesn't know me.'

She asked him to wait.

He waited. He shouldn't have added that bit about Bartos not knowing him. Lang had advised him to say the minimum. 'Keep it simple,' he had said. 'You don't want him asking you too many questions.'

A man with an Eastern European accent came on. He pronounced each word separately, distinctly and with a slight emphasis. 'Zador Bartos speaking. How can I help you, Mr McPherson?'

'I have a painting that I believe may interest you.'

There was a slight pause, as if Bartos had turned aside to indicate to the girl that he needed a pad and pen. Andy could feel him, the serious weight of his presence in his voice on the other end of the line.

'I always have time to look at paintings that will interest me, Mr McPherson. I shall be here until three this afternoon.'

'I'll call by this morning. If that's okay?'

'I shall expect you.'

He hung up. He needn't have said, *If that's okay*. Of course it was okay. He was supposed to be confident, in charge of the situation. The palm of his hand was damp with sweat. What a voice! He could imagine the owner of that voice singing the bass in a Russian church, making the candle flames tremble and the mirrors rattle. There was a beauty and a power in that man's voice. Like a well-tuned V8 idling.

He went upstairs and took a clean shirt off the pile and ironed it. He liked the smell of ironing. It reminded him of his mother. In his memory of her ironing, she was standing at the board listening to John Arlott commentating the test cricket for the BBC. It was always a summer day. A memory in which everything was calm and right with the world. In memories of his mother the sun was always shining outside.

Driving over to Armadale with the painting in the back of the station wagon, he was thinking of Lang assuring him that the painting really was a genuine Arthur Streeton. It just had one or two problems. It was up to Zador Bartos to decide whether he wanted it or not by exercising his judgement as a well-known dealer in Australian art. He didn't have to buy it. It was up to him. So what if he didn't buy it? Jo would feel easier about things. The trouble was, he wanted to succeed at this. She had been right when she said maybe he wanted to do it. He did want to do it. He wanted to do it for himself as much as for Lang. It was that man thing, wanting to prove to himself he could stand up and make it with the serious people. He might tell himself he didn't care one way or the other how it worked out, but the truth was he did care.

By the time he had parked and stepped out of the car, he was nervous again. It was the caring that made him nervous. He didn't want to walk away with his tail between his legs, carrying the picture. Struggling to get the painting out of the back of the station wagon without knocking the impressive frame, he swore under his breath. He set it down carefully on the footpath and covered it with Lang's blanket. He stood by the car and took a look around. There was one word written in ornate gilt lettering across the front door of the gallery: *Bartos*. In the centre of the window stood an easel with a landscape painting of an Australian scene resting on it. A black curtain behind the painting and the easel concealed the interior of the gallery from the street. On the city side of the gallery there was a jeweller's shop and on the other side a French-style cafe. Bartos had set himself up in the middle of one of the smartest shopping areas along the main street of one of the most affluent suburbs in Melbourne.

Andy carried the covered painting to the door of the gallery and pushed against it with his shoulder. The door opened more easily than he was expecting. A tall man wearing an expensive pinstripe suit had swung it open for him. Andy thanked him and carried the painting into the gallery. There was no one else present. He was met by the fresh smell of apples. On a small circular table there was a large white porcelain bowl filled with a carefully arranged pile of polished green apples. There were no pictures on the walls and no sign of the girl who had answered his call. A large pale wood desk stood in the far corner of the gallery on the left, behind it a closed door. Two chairs stood a little apart from the desk, a low coffee table between them, a glass ashtray in the centre of the table. On the desk was a yellow telephone handset and a carafe of water and two glasses.

The man came over and offered his hand. 'Thank you for bringing your picture. I'm Zador Bartos.' His grip was firm but not aggressive. 'Let me help you with it.' He picked up the painting without effort, carried it across the room and leaned it against the desk. Andy followed him. Zador Bartos removed Lang's old blanket and revealed the painting.

Andy and Zador Bartos stepped away from the picture and stood looking at it silently. Andy wondered if Bartos could see the restorations.

No traffic noise from the street entered the space. The silence was immense. Andy wanted to like Bartos. He found himself wanting to tell him the whole truth, give him the story. Get it out in the open. *I bought it in a broken and filthy condition a month ago at Sullivans in Bridge Road. I suppose you know that auction house.*

Bartos said, 'It is an impressive painting, Mr McPherson. Where did you get it?'

'A friend asked me to sell it for her. It's been hanging in her family's home since before she was born.'

'So why didn't your friend bring it to me?' Bartos's voice was quiet, relaxed, sounding the deep tone of the Russian Orthodox Church, a great pipe organ, sonorous, exotic, belonging to a remote world.

Andy said, 'They don't want any publicity. They don't want to be known.'

'Why is that?' Bartos's voice was soft, deep; inquiring, it seemed, from a natural interest. 'It's a little unusual, isn't it? How long have you known this friend?' He turned to Andy and met his gaze, a friendly smile lighting his large brown eyes. He was a very attractive man and gave Andy the impression of being trustworthy and honest.

'I don't know,' Andy said.

'You don't know how long you've known your friend, or you don't know why her family are suddenly in a hurry to be rid of this painting that they've had hanging on their wall for more than a generation?'

Andy's mouth had gone dry. 'Yes, I meant I don't know why they're hoping to sell it privately.'

Bartos was looking at the picture again. 'It's the kind of picture that would do well in an auction.'

Andy waited.

Bartos said, 'Did your friend tell you the price the family want for it?'

'She said I shouldn't accept less than twenty-five thousand.'

'There doesn't appear to be a signature. Did she tell you the name of the artist?'

'It's by Sir Arthur Streeton. Oh yes, and she wants the twenty-five thousand in cash.' He just managed to stop himself adding, *if that's okay.* He looked at the carafe of water on the desk.

'For how long did you say you'd known these people?'

'I didn't say, but . . .' He gagged on the dryness of his mouth. 'I couldn't get a drink of water, I suppose?'

Bartos astonished him then by placing a comforting hand on Andy's shoulder. 'I'm so very sorry, Mr McPherson. Do please forgive me.' He went around the desk and filled one of the glasses with water and brought it back and handed it to Andy.

Andy took a drink and handed the glass back to him. 'Thank you.'

Bartos said, 'So your mysterious friend wants you to sell her family's heirloom for her?' He sounded amused.

Andy didn't respond at once, but waited a few seconds before saying, 'She said if you're not interested in buying it, I should offer it to Margaret Sewell.'

'Oh, Maggie Sewell. Well, that's not a bad idea.' Bartos stepped up to the picture and crouched down to examine it closely before standing up again and pulling it away from the desk. He examined the back of the canvas and ran his finger around the inside of the frame, as if he were looking for some kind of imperfection.

The negotiation wasn't going the way Lang had told him to expect.

Bartos stood and, still facing the painting, asked, 'Have you sold many paintings for your friend before?' His voice was quiet now, steady, probing for the truth. He turned around and looked directly into Andy's eyes.

Andy looked away from him to the painting. 'Are you interested in it or not?'

Bartos permitted the hint of a smile to play about his eyes. 'We don't need to be hasty about this. But I do have to wonder why these friends of yours are in such a great hurry to be rid of their picture?' He spoke slowly, with deliberation, and as if he had given the matter a lot of thought. He was comfortable. Confident of his position. He could keep Andy there or tell him to get out and take his picture with him. 'And you say this picture has been in your friend's family for a long time. For how long exactly? Does she remember when the family purchased it? And from whom they bought it?'

'All I know is that she told me to bring it to you because you are the leading expert in the field of Australian art.'

'So is this friend of yours known to me?'

'She didn't say.'

'She didn't say.' He repeated Andy's words thoughtfully, dwelling on them. 'She doesn't seem to have said very much at all, does she? A woman of few words.' He waited for the disbelief in his tone to sink in. 'Your friend trusts you to sell an important family possession for her. But you seem to know very little about this friend, if you'll forgive me. Without a signature and no provenance, you are asking rather a lot of me.' His tone hardened a little on this last observation. 'The provenance of a painting such as this is important in determining its value, wouldn't you say?'

Andy didn't respond.

'Anonymity isn't a good idea, you know, in matters of this kind. It doesn't inspire confidence. You might mention to her that I said so.'

Andy was very uncomfortable now. Bartos clearly didn't believe a word he had told him, but was nevertheless still interested in the painting.

Bartos said quietly, 'With offers such as yours, I like to get a second opinion before making a decision. This picture is in a new frame. And it has recently been restored. Someone else, apart from your friend in whose house it has been hanging for so many years, will know about its movement from the old family home that you've mentioned. Is it all right with you if I call one of my advisers?'

'Yes, of course,' Andy said. He was beginning to feel the first stirrings of shame.

'Perhaps you'd care to sit down while I make the call.' He gestured to the chairs that stood to one side of his desk.

'It's okay,' Andy said, and remained standing. Sitting down, he could imagine himself looking like a mendicant in a waiting room, waiting for the verdict of the powerful. Sitting down would be surrendering to Bartos's greater truth. So he stood.

THE DEAL

Bartos went around the desk and sat down. He picked up the phone and made a call. Again, he spoke in the slow, considered, rumbling bass voice, like a rock slide gathering momentum down the side of a mountain, heading directly for Andy's little shack in the valley. Andy tried to make out what he was saying, but Bartos was not speaking English. He did not sound displeased, however, and kept glancing up at Andy and nodding his head. He put the phone down and said, 'How much is your friend asking, did you say?' His directness caught Andy off guard.

'As I said, she needs twenty-five thousand dollars in cash.'

Bartos's expression had tightened and a hard look had come into his eyes. Andy thought for an instant he was about to tell him to get out of his gallery and to take his painting with him.

'I don't have twenty-five thousand in cash with me, Mr McPherson.'

His contempt was humiliating.

'I can give you five thousand in cash and a cheque for the remainder. I will make the cheque out to cash if you wish.' His gaze was steady on Andy.

'Fine,' Andy said. 'Thank you.'

'And if you will let me have a receipt? I shall need it for my accountant.'

Andy's underarms were wet with sweat.

Bartos turned and went out through the door behind his desk. He closed the door after him. Andy was longing to be out of the place. He stood in the white space of the empty gallery waiting for the payoff.

Bartos came out from the back room and handed Andy a wad of fifty-dollar notes. 'You will need to count them.'

Andy took the money without speaking and shoved it into his jacket pocket.

Bartos sat at his desk and wrote out a cheque. He tore the cheque out of the book and handed it to Andy.

Andy picked up Lang's blanket and left the Bartos Gallery behind him with five thousand dollars cash in his jacket pocket and a cheque for twenty thousand. His heart was racing and his palms were sweaty. It took a great effort to open the car boot and put the blanket in there while trying to appear calm. He drove into the city and cashed Bartos's cheque and added the wad of fifties the teller handed him to the wad already in his pocket. As he drove through the heavy traffic, his thoughts were gyrating around at high speed in his head, and he was asking himself if Bartos was the crook or if the crook was himself.

He wasn't sure what he had done. Would his father really have understood? Or would he, like Jo, have seen through the kind of make-believe that renders life tolerable? Isn't idealism always defeated by life? He couldn't remember his mother ever taking an interest in art. So long as his father was happy, she was also happy. Her consolation was the occasional cigarette and a good book to get lost in and the health of her children. What was his own consolation to be without that innocence of intention which made him love and admire his father?

22

Andy and Lang went straight through to the kitchen. Mother Cat was lying in her bed, formed by a blanket and an old pillow. She looked at Andy warily but stayed in her nest. Lang went over to her and crouched down. He scratched her head with his fingers. She half closed her eyes and began to purr. He turned to Andy. 'The vet said she's getting old and won't have any more kittens. I'm giving her mineral supplements with her food. She will enjoy a peaceful old age with me.' Lang stood up. 'Do you like her?'

'She's a very lucky pussy cat.'

'Do you think she's handsome?'

'I wouldn't have said handsome, but she's quite appealing.'

'Quite appealing? See, you *are* English. I have named her Agatha.' He smiled at Andy. 'Does this shock you?'

'It does a bit. It's pretty surprising.'

'It surprised me too. I just called her Agatha one morning without thinking. I laughed at myself. It was very silly. But then I decided she had claimed the name from me. Do you believe in ghosts?'

'Not really.'

'Would you like a cup of tea? I'm afraid I can't offer you anything stronger. It's forbidden in this house. It was cursed by the Prophet. *Maledetto dal Profeta*.' He laughed, an edge of bitterness in the tone of it.

He looked lovingly at the mother cat. She was watching him. 'I have never had a cat before. But, you see, I don't have her. She has me.' He measured Andy with a long look. 'Do you think I'm going a bit senile? Since being released from the department I don't do very much. I spend a lot of time waiting and hoping. She keeps me company. She gives me something to do. I am busy looking after her. Busy waiting. She understands. My mother had a small dog. It was the same. I remember that little dog but I have forgotten its name.'

Lang filled the kettle and set it on the stove.

'So, Andy. To business.' He said this with regret and sadness. 'From love to filthy lucre. You've got the money.' It was a statement, not a question.

Andy placed the bundles of fifties on the table. 'It's all there. Twenty-five thousand. I cashed his cheque as soon as I got it.'

Lang stood looking at the money lying on the table among the auction catalogues and dirty dishes. The notes were clean and new, held in bunches of twenty with thin elastic bands. 'You did it!' He looked at Andy. 'You did it! I knew you could. You have done all the work.' He picked up a bundle and held it out to Andy. 'It is sordid. This whole transaction is sordid. But it is necessary for us to be sordid sometimes. You must at least take this.'

'No thanks.'

'Take it!'

Andy crossed the room and looked out of the window. The mother cat contracted her body but didn't leave her nest.

'Her pear tree's still hanging on.' The wilderness of Lang's garden. A feeling of mystery about it. If Lang had offered him something else, a picture from his collection, maybe he would have accepted it. But he wasn't going to take any of Bartos's money.

'I can't make you take it.' He lit a cigarette and gazed unhappily at the money on the table. 'We're not drug dealers.' He gave a hollow laugh. 'It just looks like it, doesn't it? If that kindly sergeant of police came in now, he would find me just as suspicious as my neighbours did before they eventually understood that the eccentric Chinaman living next door to them wasn't going to harm either them or the value of their house. We didn't do anything illegal, did we? It just looks suspicious. People have been convicted on the basis of appearances.'

Andy said, 'No. It's not illegal, Lang. But when I think of my father and his admiration for the watercolour landscapes of John Sell Cotman and Varley and their like, I know he would not approve of what I'm doing. I'd better get going.'

He was going home to write his notes. In his notes he would examine the curiously twisted morality of this deal in some detail. He would unknot it and lay it out for inspection. He would find some clarity about it in his own mind. But how honest would he be? And he would be sure to have something to say about Lang's look of unhappiness now that he had the money and could buy the image of the nude woman with her back to him. Andy knew with absolute certainty that Lang would be disappointed with the Sickert if he actually did manage to get hold of it. Jo had been right when she said it would solve nothing for him.

Lang's eyes had filled with tears. 'You are right, Andy.'

Andy thought he might be about to weep.

'But no one else would have done this for me.' Lang spoke meekly, as if he were one of the lost boys in his classes at the school, some parentless child wondering what life could possibly hold for him, an outsider looking in, forlorn and puzzled. At one with the lost boy who had given him the brush pot.

'It was easier than I thought it would be. I knew he wanted that picture the instant he saw it. He was pretty transparent, really, for a cagey art dealer.'

Lang said quietly, 'Bartos made a phone call while you were there. He had his doubts. But it was the phone call that decided him to buy our Streeton.'

'How do you know this?'

'Maja called me.'

'He called Maja! Jesus!'

'She told him she'd recently cleaned the Streeton and given it a new frame. She assured him it was definitely a work of Streeton's.'

'He didn't ask her who she'd done that work for?'

'He may have. She didn't say. But if he did, she would not have told him. The reason I went to Maja is that I trust her discretion. Maja and I go back a long way. She would never betray my trust. She would not consider it her business what Bartos chooses to do. Bartos can make his own mistakes.'

Andy noticed that the mother cat was watching Lang through half-closed eyes. He was sure he wouldn't be able to call her Agatha. He said, 'I have to go.'

Lang went with him to the front door. When Andy turned to say goodbye, Lang gave him a sad little smile; it was a smile that reminded Andy of the ineradicable melancholy of Lang's damaged soul, the deep loneliness of his life. They should have been celebrating with a decent bottle of wine.

When Andy drove off, Lang was still standing in the open doorway, his hand raised in a gesture of sad farewell. He looked small and vulnerable and alone standing there, above him the dragon with its folded wings glaring out from the roof at an enemy it had been powerless to overcome. When Andy turned the corner at the end of the street, he had the awful feeling that this might have been the last time he would ever see Lang.

He had an hour before he needed to pick up Hennie. He went out to the kitchen and made a coffee and took it up to his workroom at the front of the house. When he sat down at his desk he was overcome at once by a feeling of deep tiredness. He managed to write a few lines in the current notebook, number eighteen. But it was no good. He couldn't think clearly. He just didn't have the energy. He felt drained and lacked conviction for the project of the notebooks. He had trouble remembering why he was writing them. He went upstairs and lay down on the bed, just for five minutes, and fell into a deep sleep.

He was woken by the ringing of the telephone. He stumbled downstairs. It was the nurse from the creche. 'Your little Hennie is still here, Andrew. Is everything all right?'

He apologised and immediately drove down to the creche. Hennie was playing happily in the sandpit. When he picked her up she struggled and cried out repeatedly, 'Noooo!' as if he were disciplining her. He apologised to the nurse and she told him not to worry. 'It happens all the time.'

At home he carried Hennie upstairs and changed her. The phone rang. He carried her downstairs and picked up the phone. He was astonished to hear his mother's voice. She hadn't called since his father's death.

She said, 'I was in bed just now. I had an offer of death, darling. I thought I should tell you. What do you think?'

He was holding Hennie in his arms. She was staring at him as if she sensed the importance for him of this moment. He said, 'I think you probably declined it, Mum.'

'Three of the sisters from my old convent in Chantilly came to me. It was a vision, darling, not just an ordinary dream. The sisters were dressed in white habits, like angels. One stood each side of me with an arm around me and the other one stood behind me, ready to take my weight. Sister Vibia told me to fall back into her arms. *We will take care of you*, she said. It sounded just like her, the way she cared for me when I was sick as a young girl. They were my family, darling. I knew they were dead and I was surprised I could hear them. I even felt the strength of purpose in their arms. Yes, I resisted and woke up. I wanted to call and tell you.' She was silent awhile, then she said, 'Do you think I should have accepted their offer?'

He said, 'Mum, it was the best offer you're likely to get at this stage of the game.'

It was the first time Andy's mother had ever asked his advice about how to live. Only this was a question of how to die.

He heard the smile in her voice when she said, 'I knew you'd say that.'

His mother was dying. She had given him and his sisters and brother everything. He loved her. They all loved her. So why had he left them and moved to the other side of the world? He couldn't answer that. He had felt compelled. That's all.

After he got off the phone he carried Hennie out the back and sat with her at the green table. He felt deeply sad and lost. There was no chance now of ever trying to explain. It was cloudy and cool but Hennie never seemed to mind the cold. She climbed off his lap and went over to her yellow truck and sat next to it, repairing the motor or giving it a service. He was watching Hennie and thinking of his mother facing her death on the other side of the world. He remembered the smile in her eyes, her cheeky dance steps whenever she heard a lively tune on the radio. She had told him that on her first day in the convent, she was standing in the hall among the other girls in the assembly listening to the Mother Superior giving an address when her legs gave way and she fell to the ground. The Mother Superior stopped her speech to the assembly and came down off the stage. She walked up to his mother and picked her up and held her in her arms. 'Don't be afraid,' she said. 'We will take care of you. You are safe now.' And she took his mother up to her own room and put her in her own bed. And so his mother became a special child from that moment. None of the others had even seen inside the Mother Superior's private bedroom, let alone slept in her bed. Did the Mother Superior climb into the bed with her later? Or did she move his mother out to some other room when she was herself ready to occupy the bed? His mother had always referred to the nuns as her family. It was visits from the priests that terrified the girls and the nuns.

Hennie abandoned her truck and called out, 'Mum!'

23

After their evening meal, Andy returned to his workroom and was writing up his notebook. It was almost ten when the phone rang. Jo had gone up to bed an hour or more ago.

He got up and went out to the phone, expecting to hear Lang's voice. Surely he hadn't got hold of the Sickert already?

'Hi!' he said into the phone. 'How did you go?'

'Am I speaking to Andrew McPherson?'

'That's me,' Andy said, guarded now. The man sounded menacing. 'How can I help you?'

'You can help yourself, Mr McPherson. Bring the cash to us at the gallery at once or I shall come around and get it. You won't like that.'

'I haven't got it.'

'Get it! You've got one hour. If you are not here with the cash by eleven, we'll come to your house and find it ourselves.' The man sounded very sure of himself. And very menacing.

'I'll see what I can do.'

Andy put the phone down and stood looking at it. He was afraid. 'Shit!'

Jo called, 'Who was it?'

He went upstairs. Jo looked at him as he came into the bedroom. She had been reading; her book was lying facedown on the blanket. 'What's up? Who was that?'

'It was some goon of Bartos's. He told me to bring the cash back tonight or else.'

'What did you tell him?'

'I said I'd see what I could do. They'll come round here within the hour if I don't take it back.'

Jo just laughed. 'Don't be silly. Of course they won't. They're just trying to scare you.'

'Well, they succeeded. I don't want them coming round here and beating the shit out of me.'

'It's rubbish. Forget it! If they call you again, tell them to get fucked. You can do that. I've heard you.' She gave him a lovely serene smile. 'Don't look so worried. They're bluffing. Bartos made his decision and bought the picture on his own judgement.'

He frowned at her. 'How come you're so bloody calm?'

'Think about it for half a minute. Maybe he found out about the painting's history and wants to renegotiate the price, but you cashing the cheque has prevented him from cancelling it. He didn't expect that. He thought you were a soft touch. He'd have got the picture for five thousand instead of twenty-five if you'd banked the cheque. You said you were a bit surprised that he didn't try to negotiate with you about the price. He didn't care because he was planning all along to cancel the cheque. But that didn't work, so now he's trying to frighten you into giving him the money back. He's still negotiating the deal. He hasn't given up yet. If you took the twenty-five thousand back to him now, he'd offer you a glass of whisky, shake your hand and tell you he'd do his best to sell the picture and would give you half of the proceeds or something like that.' She picked up her book and said dismissively, 'It's obvious. You're not a crook. You don't think like them. You think negotiations are asking someone to take a bit off the price of something. That's not what these people do.'

'How the fuck do you know all this?'

She looked up from her book and smiled at him. It was the smile she had given him on the bus to Sydney all those years back. 'You're an innocent. I just *know*. Bartos and his people have just proved they're crooks; I'm relieved you and Lang haven't ripped off some poor honest person. I'll bet you they'll sell it to someone else for a massive profit.'

'You're amazing.'

'If they dared to come around here and force their way in it would be in the paper and on the news in the morning. They would be announcing to the Melbourne art world that they really are crooks, which probably everyone already knows. I don't think they're going to risk their reputation, do you? That's more important than this.' She reached for his hand and held it. 'I'd love to hear you telling them to get fucked.'

He sat down on the side of the bed and they leaned towards each other and kissed. Her lips were warm and soft. 'God, I love you!' he said.

'Get into bed! You're letting cold air in.'

'I'll wait till the hour's up. I don't want to be caught with my pants down.'

24

They heard nothing more from Bartos and his henchman, and not a word from Lang. Life went on for Jo and Andy and Hennie without any drama, and the deal for the most part drifted into the background.

Then, three weeks later, Lang called.

Jo answered the phone and, without greeting her or inquiring after Hennie, he asked to speak to Andy. It was Lang's way, to bypass Jo. She found it amusing rather than affronting. 'I'll get him,' she said. 'He's out in the garden with Hennie.'

Lang said, 'Thank you.'

When they had met, Lang had been aware that evening that Jo saw him as Chinese, while she saw Andy, also a migrant, as Australian. It was the way most people had seen him and he didn't expect this to change. Usually he didn't care. But every now and then something came up that made his exclusion seem important and hurtful to him. He had found formality, the mask of personal dignity, to be the safest solution.

Jo waited a second or two, and when it was clear Lang had no more to say, she set the phone on the table and went out to the back garden. Andy was lying on his stomach on the patch of grass in the late sun while Hennie tottered unsteadily towards him, her arms flapping like immature wings, her fat legs taking her forward for a step or two then sending her swerving off to one side. She corrected her direction and came on towards where Andy was lying with his arms stretched out towards her, ready for her to throw herself into his embrace. Jo stood and watched till Hennie reached him and she and Andy were rolling around in each other's arms laughing. Then she said, 'Lang's on the phone.'

Andy disentangled himself from Hennie and handed her over to Jo. Hennie objected strongly and Andy hesitated, but Jo said, 'Just go! She'll be right the minute you're out of sight.'

He went down the passage and picked up the phone. 'Did you get it?'

'Yes.'

'Well, that's great, Lang. You must be thrilled.'

'Can you come over?'

'Of course. I can't wait to see it.'

Andy went back out to the garden. Jo was sitting at the green table with Hennie on her lap. They were engrossed in a finger game. She looked at Andy. 'Did he get the Sickert?'

'Yes, he's got it.'

'Are you going over there now?'

He leaned down and they kissed and then he kissed Hennie. 'I'll see you later.' He added, 'For someone who's just realised his life's dream he sounded very ordinary.'

When Andy turned into Lang's street, he saw Lang standing under the light at his front door watching for him.

Andy parked and stepped over the wall and headed along the worn track through the grass. When he reached the door, Lang didn't say anything but turned around and led him into the front sitting room. A small unframed canvas lay on its back beside the vase of dead hydrangeas on the table under the window. The blue folder was open beside it, the Sickert drawing that Lang had shown him a few weeks back displayed.

They went over and stood by the table. 'So that's it,' Andy said.

'That's it.' Lang drew deeply on his cigarette. He laughed, a hollow kind of self-mockery. He sucked hard on the cigarette, then was caught suddenly by a paroxysm of coughing.

Andy thought the unframed canvas rather shabby. It was the kind of blobby-looking heavy painting his father had disliked. Neither one thing nor the other. An idea. Maybe an obsession. Some intention half realised. The disfiguring lust of the artist's eye distorting the woman's vulnerable nakedness. The woman was not admired by this artist but had been scrubbed vigorously onto the canvas with a kind of angry frustration.

Lang recovered with a final clearing cough. 'You don't like it.'

'I can't say I do.' Those dark acres of heavy flesh would depress him if he had to look at them every day. The woman's form was backlit from a window with a flimsy curtain over it. Her features were hidden. A great mop of hair straggling over her shoulders. She was standing side-on, more towards the window than the viewer, her left breast looming out of her chest. Dark it was, no living flesh tones to delight the eye but indistinct grey mounds with shimmering edges caught in the window's half-light. There was a weight, a kind of reluctance, about the heaviness of the figure and the way the painting was so indistinctly lit. Andy's impression was of something held back, a refusal to reveal the intention in the painter's mind, or perhaps a conscious desire to keep his intention concealed, a suggestion of coarseness and deceit, which he didn't like but which he could see might suit Lang's own masked existence, his perverse way of approaching the truth, as if truth might be disputed and made to look less true. He could see why Sickert had played such an important role in Lang's life.

Andy turned to him. 'You don't seem to be ecstatic about it yourself.'

'I picked it up from Simon last night. As soon as I got it home and unwrapped it I remembered Simon's nervous manner when he first offered to show it to me.' He looked at Andy. 'Why did I buy a painting with no provenance? I know better than to do that. I didn't even question him. I was bowled over by it that day at his gallery. I wanted to be looking at something in his back room that was totally inaccessible to me.' He laughed again. 'I was after the Holy Grail, Andy, and I wanted to believe I'd found it.' He stabbed at the picture with his index finger the way he had stabbed at his portrait of Agatha, as if he were accusing the painting of something for which he lacked words. 'That's it. It's mine now. And now I've started thinking. When Simon showed it to me that day in his back room I didn't think. I just wanted it.'

They both stood there looking down at the picture of the naked form of the woman.

Lang said sadly, 'I need a drink, Andy.' There was not only sorrow in his expression but also a wistful regret. And when he said, 'Why is everything good in my life taken from me?' it was with puzzlement, but without bitterness.

Andy said nothing.

'Simon's anonymous family wouldn't settle for twenty-five. I had to borrow another ten from Sergei. I've never borrowed money before. I handed over thirty-five thousand dollars in cash to Simon and he gave me this canvas. I knew at once that I had just done the stupidest thing in my life. But until I got home with it I hung on to the faint hope that it would work its magic for me.' He smoked his cigarette and looked at the picture. 'It's no wonder Agatha left me. I would have left me if I'd had any sense.' He laughed unhappily.

'You sound as if you're sure it's a fake now?' Andy said. He would have quite liked a drink himself.

'Sure? No, I'm not sure, not of anything. How can I be? I might be an obsessive and a failure but I'm not insensitive. Simon did tell me something, however, that will interest you. It concerns us both. We were having a cup of tea and smoking in his back room and he was filling me in on the trade gossip. He said he had heard from a London contact that Bartos had sold an important Heidelberg School painting to an Australian multinational for their London boardroom. He didn't say how much this fabled painting went for, but it was evidently a very good price.'

'Did Simon connect it with you?'

'Oh no! It was just a bit of gossip.'

'Are you sure it was ours?'

'That I *am* sure of. And you know what? It was signed.'

'Jesus! Who would have signed it?'

'I think we both know the answer to that. If that Streeton ever comes up for auction in one of the big London houses, its provenance will be thoroughly researched before it's catalogued. The research will stop with us. Bartos will swear it was signed when he bought it from us. Why, he would ask reasonably, would a reputable dealer like himself purchase an unsigned painting without any provenance? I will be accused of having signed it, and you and I will be charged with forgery and fraud. This possibility is going to haunt our futures. Bartos will not be unmasked. It is you and I, Andy, who will be required to wear this one.' He stabbed his finger at the nude again. 'Was she worth it?' He laughed and coughed. 'Think about it. Was she worth it?' He seemed to be genuinely amused.

He stubbed his cigarette out in the glass ashtray and lit a fresh one. 'Sickert is the most frequently faked British artist. I knew that. I've always known it. He was widely faked in his own day. When he returned to England after living in France, a friend took him to an exhibition of Sickert's work at a gallery somewhere in the West End. The works were all fakes. Sickert took a good look at them and said they were very good. He did nothing about it. He was a strange man, gifted and unusual; some people even suggested he was a serial killer.'

'You don't actually seem all that depressed about this,' Andy observed. 'Anyway, Maja saw the Streeton when it was unsigned. If your faith in her is justified, she will testify that the picture was not signed when it left your hands. It would be her word against that of Bartos. Bartos would not risk a public stoush over it. He'd just deny signing it and it would remain a mystery. There is no evidence that you signed it and I would have been incapable of forging a Streeton signature.'

'If I seem to be a bit fatalistic about it then it's probably because I was half expecting this. Nothing else has ever really worked out for me, has it? So why should this so-called Sickert have delivered me from my despair?'

'Despair's a bit strong, isn't it? You don't strike me as someone in despair.'

'Do you know many people in despair? What does despair look like to you? There may be an outward calm and acceptance about it, don't you think? You are the writer. Anyway, the story's not over yet. I'll send a high-quality colour slide of the painting to Amanda Forsyth in London. She wrote the book on Sickert's forgeries. I've got a copy of it here somewhere. She's a consultant at the British Museum.' He chuckled. 'I'm pretty confident I know what she'll say.'

25

Days and weeks went by and Jo and Andy were preoccupied with the rapid changes in their daughter. Hennie had begun to utter a few words, or at least to make sounds which Jo and Andy claimed they recognised as words. They had great faith in the little genius they had produced between them.

It was late on Friday evening and Jo was carrying Hennie up to bed. Hennie was fast asleep, exhausted from playing on the rug in the sitting room for the last hour.

Andy was behind Jo, his foot on the first step of the stair, when he paused and said, 'I think I'll give Mum a ring.'

Jo went on and Andy stepped back and sat at the table under the stairs. He picked up the phone and called his mother's number. His brother Harry picked up on the first ring. 'Oh, it's you!' he said. 'I thought it must have been the hospital calling again. Mum just passed away, literally a minute ago.'

A sob engulfed Andy and he was unable to speak.

Harry said, 'Sorry, Andy. Call me later. It's okay. I was going to ring you. It's amazing you rang just then.'

Andy hung up and sat with his head in his hands. He wept helplessly for a couple of minutes. When he'd gathered himself he went out to the kitchen and drank a glass of water. The last time he'd wept as helplessly as this was when his mother had called to tell him his father had died. The moment of death seemed to carry with it an enormous punch of pure grief. It had come to him each time as a shock and was quite different from the sadness of knowing his mother was dying. Now she was dead. The door had slammed. He stood in the kitchen sipping a second glass of water and looking out into the night garden. His mother had told him she'd been woken in the night by the fierce sound of his father's voice crying out her name, 'Winnie!' shouted into her ear in the night. Harry was staying with her at that time. She had sat up and called him in and told him, 'Your father has just gone.' A moment later the hospital rang with the news. Now his mother had called to him! He was sure of it. Why else would he have decided on an impulse to call her? He rarely called her, and almost never last thing in the evening. He asked himself once again why he had left her when he was a boy and gone to the other side of the world.

He put down the glass and went through to the stairs and walked up step by step, the strangeness swirling in his brain, the question that always defeated him. He went into the bedroom.

Jo set her book aside. 'What is it?'

'My mum just died.' He undressed and climbed into bed with Jo and she held him in her arms. He wept again. The strength of his grief surprised him. Something powerful that had lain silently in him all his life had been woken by his mother's death. He said, 'I didn't think I'd be so affected.'

'Of course you're deeply affected, darling. How could you not be?'

'But I'm not alone. When Harry said she'd just died I felt totally alone. As if she was all I had ever had. Now gone. It's crazy. I don't think there's very much that I've ever really understood.'

They lay silently in each other's arms.

'Do you think she really called to me at the moment of her passing?'

'Of course she did. You were her lost son.'

26

It was a Monday. Andy was in his workroom transcribing his notebooks onto the typewriter when he heard the postie rattling around at the letterbox. The manuscript had grown steadily to over a hundred and fifty pages and he could not see an end to it. He waited till the postie moved on then went out and checked the box. There was a letter from Lang. He stood at the front gate looking at the writing on the envelope. Lang had lovely handwriting. It was unmistakable, full of character and learning, with a quiet kind of confidence that spoke of the man's modesty and, despite his bohemian past, belief in good manners. A neat flowing hand in blue ink.

THE DEAL

Andy went back inside the house and closed the front door on the roar of the traffic. He stood in the half-light of the passage and opened the envelope. It was a long letter. It began:

> My dear and only true friend,
> By the time you receive this letter I shall be dead. The time for me to use the rifle has arrived. I am calm and sure of the rightness of what I am doing. When you said that day of the Sickert nude that I didn't seem to be too bothered by the wreck of this endeavour of ours, you were right. I had seen already that it was time for me to bring my fruitless struggle to an end. I was feeling quietly liberated from the endless anxiety and suffering of these past few years. I haven't been drinking. I am calm and sober. To continue would be for me to choose to go on with the pointlessness of it all. I am tired, Andy. I want to be done with it.

Andy groaned aloud with the horror of it. But, strangely, it was not sorrow but anger that most moved him. Why hadn't Lang called on him? He didn't stop reading while these thoughts were jostling for room in his brain.

> My forebears here were never ghetto Chinese. They married with the Irish and the Scots and the English and have lived among the general Australian community since 1848. With an Irish mother and a Scottish father you were ready-made for this place. I have concluded that I am

Chinese and I am ready to meet my ancestors. I remember everything about my childhood. I shall return to the little red door where my mother will be waiting for me.

There is something I must ask you to do. Would you please rescue Mother Cat from my garden. If she is left there to fend for herself she will be tormented by the aggressive male cats that roam around at night. You and Jo can give her a good life. I know you will do this.

Farewell, dear friend. Please don't hate me for this. I know it is the most sensible solution for me. Without the solace of drink my life is not worth living.

I've enclosed Amanda Forsyth's reply. I have no further use for it. You should know what she says. And who knows? It may come in useful.

Andy unfolded the blue airmail letter. The letterhead was the British Museum, lightly embossed.

Dear Mr Tzu,
Thank you for your inquiry and for the inclusion of the slide. Your painting is known to me. I am most interested to hear that it has surfaced in Australia. As far as we know, and despite numerous inquiries over the years, your painting is the only example of a work purporting to be by Sickert which is evidently based on the pencil study in the photocopy, which I've included here for your information. The pencil study is in our holdings here at the British Museum and is a known work by Walter Richard Sickert.

You notice in your letter that I do not include a reference to your painting in my book. Sickert forgeries of quality have become over the years a genre of their own and are widely collected. There is such a great number of these paintings in circulation that I had to restrict my research exclusively to paintings that we were able to establish as definite forgeries. Many others of uncertain provenance abound, however, and another study of these paintings may well become the subject of a future book.

The problem with your painting is that, despite numerous attempts over the years by a variety of well-respected English dealers and scholars to establish a reliable provenance for it, doubts stubbornly cling to it. This is, in my opinion, the principal reason for its disappearance from the market in the UK, more than twenty years ago now. I'm afraid I'm not in a position to assure you that your painting is a forgery or that it is in fact a painting by the hand of Sickert himself. The last search I undertook for the whereabouts of your painting ended for me in Albuquerque in New Mexico. But that is a very long time ago now . . .

Jo was upstairs changing Hennie. He went up and, when she had finished pinning the nappy, he handed the letter to her. 'He's shot himself.' He waited, watching for her reaction. 'It was posted Friday evening. He must have been totally serious to make sure I wouldn't come charging over there to talk him out of it.'

Jo was sitting on the side of the bed reading the letter, her hand to her mouth. She looked up and held out a hand to him. 'I'm so sorry.'

He took her hand and held it. He wasn't going to weep. Death was death, but his strongest emotion just then was a mixture of anger and guilt.

Jo said, 'You'd better go over there.'

'What good will that do?'

'You'll have to find the mother cat. You'll have to buy a cat carrier on the way. Take one of our old towels and make it a bit comfortable for her.'

'She might not be easy to catch. She's still wary of me.'

'You'll never forgive yourself if you don't try.' She stood up and embraced him. 'There's no more you could have done for him. Think of it, it's not such a bad decision for him. Sometimes suicide makes sense.'

He drove over to Lang's. The bay window to Lang's bedroom was covered by two sheets of corrugated iron. The police must have been alerted and smashed their way in. He stood looking at it. The bow window to the left was the window of the front room, where the portrait of Agatha hung above the fireplace and Berat's brush pot and the vase of dead hydrangeas stood on the mahogany table.

Andy stepped in over the wall and peered in through the left-hand window. The sitting room was empty. A vacant space.

Someone had cleaned it out. There was no furniture and no sign of Agatha's portrait. Who had taken all of Lang's things? There was a whole life Andy knew nothing about. It was a weird feeling looking into that bare room, a feeling that he might have dreamed the whole thing.

He went back to the car and picked up the cat carrier. He sat in the passenger seat, the cat carrier on his knees, and stared at the house, the dragon with its hooded eyes gazing out. The silence of the street. The terrible absence. The words of a childhood nursery rhyme that his mother had sung to him came into his head. He was compelled to speak the words aloud: *'Who killed Cock Robin? I, said the sparrow, with my bow and arrow. I killed Cock Robin.'*

THE TIME OF GHOSTS

27

May 2023. Andy is eighty-seven.

My Hennie will arrive later today. It will be her forty-eighth birthday tomorrow. We shall celebrate together. I will go down to the station ten minutes before her train is due. The train from Melbourne is reliably either ten minutes late or ten minutes early. It seems to be a rule of the railway system to avoid having it arrive on time. They like to surprise us, I suppose. Or perhaps it is to keep us in suspense. Every once in a while, just to let us know they can do it if they really want to, they permit the train to arrive precisely on time. On those occasions they behave as if this is normal.

I must remember to tell Hennie my dream! I am inclined to get sidetracked and forget the main thing these days. Hennie says this is not new and insists that I have always been like that.

Lang's suicide haunted me. I have lived with him close to my heart ever since. When I at last went to China to search for evidence of his mother's fate, there were moments when I felt I was Lang—especially the day I climbed to the temple of Ling Yin in Hangzhou. My friend and companion that day was Professor Hwang. It was he who told me I must visit the temple on my own. *It is the temple of the soul's retreat*, he said. *Lang's mother's ghost may have found peace there. You will know when you are there.* It poured with rain all that day, water cascading down the ancient stone steps, the bamboo forest bent low as if kowtowing to the spirit of the storm. The old spirit of China was still very much alive in that place. The magic of West Lake on a winter evening, the arched bridge shrouded in mist, the water still as ice. I remembered Lang asking me if I believed in ghosts.

Climbing those sacred steps to the temple I believed in ghosts. And I still believed then that I might have saved him and that I bore some responsibility for his despair. It was my darling Jo, of course, who finally convinced me that Lang's decision had been the right one for him. Jo possessed a quality of wisdom that has eluded me. It was the wisdom to see to the bedrock of things and to state the truth with clarity. *It is a rare gift*, she said, *to know when it is time for us to leave. Lang knew and had the courage and the means to do it. For him it was right.* I say she finally convinced me, but that is not quite true. A feeling of guilt and responsibility for his decision to die still lingers in my mind. It will never quite leave me. I don't know whether it is justified or not, I just know it is there and I feel it.

I did write his story. There was a necessity in that project for me. The book, in the end, gave me a certain local fame when it finally came out. I could not bear to have him dead in my account and so I lied and brought him back to life. I was thanked for this. But it was a book not so much about Lang, after all, as a celebration of the loss of our ancestral homelands. The freedoms from custom we enjoy, the freedoms of the cosmopolitan mind and heart, after all, are what we of the modern world have exchanged for the antique traditions and duties of home. Has it been a fair exchange? The loss of an ancestral home, the music and the dance of our deep forebears, is most often lamented by those of us who enjoy freedom from the ancient constraints of kinship. I set out to write the plain truth of Lang's fate here, but after many years the memory had made a fiction of the myriad facts. The questions remained unanswered.

I would like to have written Agatha's story, but she resisted my imagination and her fate remained closed to me. So in a ghostly way, intimate to the imagination and melancholy of the nearness of death now, she endures in my mind, more present because less accounted for than Lang.

Hennie and I and Jo enjoyed Mother Cat's presence with us for seven years. I don't know how old she was when Lang died. Perhaps she was eight. But she was in her old age when she had her final collapse. The vet thought she might be fifteen or sixteen. Cats can live longer than this, of course, but she'd had a tough life as a young cat and no doubt had mothered numerous kittens. Hennie helped me dig a grave beside the silver birch and we buried her there. I wrapped her in my favourite towel. Hennie and I were in tears as we laid her little body in the ground. Jo, if I remember rightly, didn't weep but stood by and watched us, moved by Hennie's tears. I still miss Mother Cat, and Hennie and I often speak of her. I don't have a cat these days. I have sometimes thought of getting one. But then I think of Mother Cat and I know she would lose her unique place with me if I were to fall in love with another cat. It would be a betrayal. Hennie says I'm ridiculous. She's right. But it's the way I am. The way I have become.

I have reached an age at which the dead have returned to me, their presence in some wonderful way more powerful and real even than it was before they died, the complications of our old relationships resolved. Today the ghosts of my past years are with me. Jo will never leave my side now. I lost her when she died and I despaired then and wept for her. For a long time she was absent from me and it was terrible. Then she returned. I speak to her freely these days as I cook my meals and vacuum the house, and when I'm working at my latest book she calls out that the coffee is ready, and then we sit together in our sunroom at the back of this house and we drink our coffee and eat Anzac biscuits and we laugh and share the best of our memories. I don't wish to replace any of my beloved dead. I've not had a new partner. Have I, in this, become like Lang with his loyalty to Agatha? If we leave their room in our hearts unoccupied, our beloved dead eventually find their way home. My mother told me this, but I was too young then to know what she meant.

The sun is shining and it's going to be hot later. I don't need a coat when I walk down to the railway station. I sit on one of the benches on Platform 1 and look at the tall poplars over behind the Railway Hotel, their leaves semaphoring to each other. The smell of coal smoke is from the vintage train. It must have just left for its pretend journey into the past. I've never taken that journey. To take it would be to spoil the mystery of its destination. But I am glad that other people take it. Hennie's train is seven minutes late. It should be here very soon. I brought with me Mark Rothko's little book, *The Artist's Reality*, to read while I waited. Almost the first thing his son, Christopher Rothko, says in his introduction is, *Some of the book's aura no doubt came from my father, although little of it directly.* Which is true for me and for my work. On reading these words of Mark Rothko's son, I felt they were written for my benefit. My father's art was unlike Rothko's and Lang's tormented gift, but remained a healing and innocent distraction for him from the brutal realities of the war. For me his art has always been a quiet gift.

Two people have begun screaming at each other at the far end of the platform. No doubt they will jump into the Quiet Carriage without noticing it is the Quiet Carriage and will continue to have their row there. Their screams drown out Rothko, and I close his book, saving his tortured contemplations on art for another time. The people who are screaming are quite smartly dressed and look to be in good health. The man is wearing bright red shoes. The woman is rolling a smoke. She looks up and screams something incoherent at him whenever he gets too close to her. She is like an irate parrot, and he a dog that teases her mercilessly.

The arrival of the train is being announced over the PA system. I stand up and ease my joints. I stiffen when I sit too long. Here it comes, sounding its shrill warning. Last night I dreamed my father came to see me. It was a vivid visitation. Detailed and real. We embraced and he said, 'It's nearly your time, son.' I knew what he meant. He looked as I do now. It was very moving for me but was not at all sad.

ACKNOWLEDGEMENTS

It has been my great good fortune to enjoy the loyal support and confidence for the past twenty-four years of my publisher and friend, Annette Barlow. My thanks are also due to Ali Lavau and Tom Bailey-Smith for their tireless attention to detail.

ALEX MILLER is the award-winning author of fourteen novels and a collection of essays and stories. He is published internationally and widely in translation. Miller is twice winner of the Miles Franklin Literary Award, for *The Ancestor Game* and for *Journey to the Stone Country*. He is an overall winner of the Commonwealth Writers Prize in 1993 for *The Ancestor Game*. *Conditions of Faith* and *Lovesong* are both winners of the Christina Stead Prize for Fiction in the NSW Premier's Literary Awards. *Landscape of Farewell* was awarded the Manning Clark Medal for Miller's outstanding contribution to Australian cultural life and the Chinese Best Foreign Novel Award, 2008. *Autumn Laing* received the Melbourne Prize for Literature, and *Coal Creek* the Victorian Premier's Literary Award. Miller's first work of non-fiction, *Max*, was shortlisted for the National Biography Award in 2021. *A Kind of Confession*, his collected letters and diaries, was published in 2023.

alexmiller.com.au